RED FIRE

RED FIRE

A Western Trio

Max Brand

Skyhorse Publishing

First Skyhorse Publishing edition published 2015 by arrangement with Golden West Literary Agency

Skyhorse Publishing books may be purchased in bulk at special discounts for sales promotion, corporate gifts, fund-raising, or educational purposes. Special editions can also be created to specifications. For details, contact the Special Sales Department, Skyhorse Publishing, 307 West 36th Street, 11th Floor, New York, NY 10018 or info@skyhorsepublishing.com.

Skyhorse® and Skyhorse Publishing® are registered trademarks of Skyhorse Publishing, Inc.®, a Delaware corporation.

Visit our website at www.skyhorsepublishing.com.

10 9 8 7 6 5 4 3 2 1

Library of Congress Cataloging-in-Publication Data is available on file.

Cover design by Brian Peterson

Print ISBN: 978-1-63450-431-7
Ebook ISBN: 978-1-5107-0041-3

Printed in the United States of America

TABLE OF CONTENTS

Master and Man

"Master and Man," which appeared in the January 5, 1924 issue of
Street & Smith's *Western Story Magazine*, is an unusual story since there
were no black heroes in pulp magazines in the 1920s. But in "Master
and Man" the real hero of the story is a black man named Bobbie,
who not only can outride, outfight, and outshoot any white man in the
mountain desert, but whose unwavering moral code serves as a model
for his often cruel and dissolute white master.

I

In his bare feet he was six feet three and a half inches in height.
He weighed two hundred and twenty pounds. He could carry
that weight over a hundred yards in ten seconds flat. He could
jump over a bar as high as the top of his head. He could throw
a sixteen-pound hammer fifty-five yards. And at Jefferson
Thompson's place, in the old blacksmith shop, ten good men
and true saw him lift a canvas sack filled with iron junk off the
floor and onto a scale, and those scales registered twelve hundred
pounds, the weight of a sizable horse.

His body was made not bulkily, but with smoothly sloping
muscles, fitted one to another so deftly that his bared arm looked
round and fat, almost like the arm of a woman. His limbs tapered
to narrow, long hands and feet. He had the head of a Greek, with
features chiseled with infinite care and strength—a long, high
nose, a square, clipped chin, and big, confident, black eyes. His
hair was like waving smoke, and his skin was as black as jet.

Such was Bobbie. Had he been white, he would have been one of the famous figures of the community, the very pride of western Texas. But, as it was, he was only the Farnsworth Negro, Bobbie. In fact, his great size, his singular skill in many ways, which enabled him to crush the rebellion out of a vicious mustang, or to throw a rope with either hand, or to work two revolvers at the same time at two different targets—all of these assets were lost sight of and forgotten in the damning phrase: "The Farnsworth Negro." The more formidable and exceptional he was, the more shameful it was considered that he should be treated like a slave. Apparently he freely accepted that treatment, which culminated on the famous occasion when his young master, Thomas Gainsborough Farnsworth, struck the big Negro squarely in the face with his fist and then beat him with his riding quirt in front of everybody in the town of Daggett. The occasion was an ugly one. Old Tom Farnsworth, who knew that his boy was wasting his time and squandering his money in a poker game in Daggett, reinforcing his waning spirits with bootleg whiskey from time to time, sent Bobbie in to give Thomas, Jr. a message that he must come home at once. Bobbie arrived just as the game was breaking up, and young Tom was sick and worried because his wallet, which had been fat, was now empty, and his future was mortgaged with certain IOUs. So he flew into a passion and beat the Negro soundly with his fists and his quirt.

Bobbie was seen to endure this punishment without stirring so much as a muscle of his face, even when Tom, maddened by his own brutality, struck Bobbie squarely across the mouth with a lash of the quirt. There was neither complaint nor dodging on the part of Bobbie. The next day big Sam Chalmers and his brother Jud, acting on the principle that a man who would endure such treatment at the hands of another must be a cur at heart, started to harry and worry Bobbie through the streets of the town of Daggett. Bobbie gave them the slip and went to the house of the sheriff.

"Sheriff Morgan," he said, "the Chalmers boys are bothering me some."

The sheriff looked with curious contempt at the huge body and the handsome face of the Negro, marked with great bars and wales by the beating of the day before.

"Can't you take care of yourself, Bobbie?" he asked. "Do I got to put you in a cage, by gum, to keep you from being spoiled?"

"Sheriff Morgan," said the big fellow, "I only want your permission to protect myself."

"Say, man," said the sheriff, whose heart was as big as his hand and as tough, "do you got to ask me for that?"

"I am a Negro," said Bobbie.

At this the sheriff dismissed Bobbie, but he remained thoughtful after his visitor had departed. Through a window he beheld Bobbie encounter the Chalmers stalwarts. Both of these men were proven fighters. They went at their quarry with a rush, and the sheriff scratched his chin as he watched them split upon Bobbie like water on a reef. They rushed at him again. Sam drew a gun, and Jud whipped out a knife, and then Bobbie struck once with either hand. That was the end of the battle. Sam was carried to the next house with a broken rib, and Jud was dragged to the same place with a shattered jaw bone.

"The big feller don't know his strength," said the town of Daggett. But, thereafter, it grew more and more curious and more and more disgusted with Bobbie. If he were truly fearless, as it seemed to be proven, what could have kept him in the service of the Farnsworth family, enduring such insult and brutality as Tom had used toward him?

The explanation requires a backward look to a day when Bobbie was only ten years old. On that occasion his old grandfather, with black skin growing gray and dusty with age, talked to him while they sat, fishing, under a willow tree. The source of the complaint was that little Bobbie was making serious objections to certain things that were required of him. Why, he had asked, should he have to polish the boots of his master? Why should young Tom be privileged to use him like a dog? Why should he, Bobbie, with more strength and adroitness in a minute than young master Tom had in a year, be forced to sit back and play second fiddle to the white boy? Other Negroes did not have to. They were free. They claimed a right to life, liberty, and property. They could swagger as boldly as any white. What was the distinction, then, between Bobbie and the rest? These were the thoughts of Bobbie, if not almost his words, and his grandfather responded with much deliberation, but smoothly, as one who speaks of that which he has long pondered.

"Bobbie," he said, "the difference between you and them is that they're growin' up to be fool niggers, and you is growin' up to be a wise one. I'll tell you a little story. You set down and rest yore feet and look at that slap-daddle water dog, lying off yonder on that stone."

"But, oh, Granddaddy," cried the little black boy, "why should we live like slaves?"

"How you go talkin', honey," said the old man, chuckling hoarsely. "Is settin' here, fishin' and squintin' at the sky through the trees, and watchin' of the ripples that come wigglin' on the bank . . . is that bein' a pore slave?" He shook his old gray head.

Here he launched into the body of his story that related how, in the old days when the Civil War passed across the land, he had remained with his master as a servant through the midst of the battling, and how he had fought at the side of the colonel, when it might be said that he was helping to tighten the rivets of the shackles that bound his own people. Afterward, when the war ended, and he and the colonel went back to the old place in Texas with their scars and their honors, he had served the bankrupt family for years after, years without a cent of pay, laboring and struggling night and day until at the last fortune changed. They moved into the western part of the state, and luck favored the colonel in the cow industry. He became wealthy. But he never could have crossed the dark hour of his life after the war had it not been for the devotion of the old Negro.

"Hisself was what said it," crooned that old toothless black man. "He said that I done help an' saved him."

He continued his narrative with the growth to manhood of his only surviving child Charlie—how Charlie came to maturity with his head full of ideas of independence; how he went to school and fought to distinguish himself; how he left the Texas ranch and journeyed across the country to New York; how he grew fat and well-to-do in that far-off city; how he married, and how Bobbie was born; how misfortune and sickness robbed Charlie of his wife and all his property; how he dragged himself back to the old ranch, sick and with his little son in his hand; how he died wishing that he had never stirred beyond the peace and safety of his home ranch in the dear old Lone Star State.

"He'd done gone and been a fool nigger," concluded the old grandfather. "And every nigger is a fool that tries to live like what a white man does. Let them lead, and we'll foller. Let them talk, and we'll work. They know, Bobbie. And them that know is a heap better and stronger than them that can only work."

Such were the opinions of his grandfather, expressed with a solemnity that amazed and subdued Bobbie. He had argued as well as he could, but it was like questioning a prophet. The old man felt he knew the truth, and he began to roar and thunder like a preacher in a church. So Bobbie had it worked firmly home in his brain that, no matter what chanced, it was better to stay faithful to a white master than to be free, because some people were meant for freedom and others were meant to be in service all their days. Such was the opinion of the grandfather.

"Them that looks high, stubs their toes and falls on their faces," he declared.

He had the glaring example of Bobbie's very own father with which to fortify his remarks, and from this example Bobbie could not escape. As for cruelty and injustice, now and again it was much better for a Negro to endure it than to strike out on his own behalf. For in the end woe and misery would be very apt to come to him. To endure the dangers of life required, said the grandfather, the adroitness of a snake and the fierceness of a hawk, and only the white man possessed these qualities of the brain. Far, far better to rest an arm upon him than to struggle for oneself.

Such was the opinion that he forced Bobbie to accept. But it was not a matter of one interview only. They talked the matter over time and time again. Little Bobbie had a thousand tests of the case. He could not reconcile himself to the manifest injustice of his grandfather's advice for a while, but in time he began to feel the weight of the old man's experience and will. In a year or so the creed had entered his mind as firmly as a religious faith, with a religious emotion behind it. If he were true to the Farnsworths, he felt, the Farnsworths would be true to him, and thus his happiness would be secured. More than this: to be faithful to the Farnsworths became more than duty and good sense. To have displeased them would have been to have committed sacrilege. Old Thomas Gainsborough Farnsworth, Sr., was a distant idol to be worshipped by Bobbie. But the immediate goal of his affections and his humble admiration was young Tom.

Young Tom grew into a slender fellow, with some wit, more sarcasm, and fists as free and ready as his tongue. He had a sallow skin and a lean, thoughtful look. In dress, like every Farnsworth, he was something of a dandy. Altogether he was a dapper young exquisite, with a cultivated taste for leisure, cards, and books. He read everything, digesting it as fast as it was devoured by his eyes, and filing it away in a memory that could forget nothing. He read, moreover, with tremendous speed. By the time he was fifteen he had crowded into his young brain more historical information of various and sundry sorts than the average college professor could boast. The result was that when he went to a great Eastern university, the first thing he did was to contract the bad habit of despising his instructors. At seventeen he could talk freely about *Critique of Pure Reason*, for he had digested the thought of the difficult old German as readily as some children see to the heart of chess problems and bewilder older opponents.

Like most prodigies, young Tom soon promised to come to a no-good end. He did not have to attend lectures in order to earn good marks. If he dodged classes, his examinations were always brilliant. His father, reading the flattering reports, decided that his boy was making a record for himself and acquiring a good and growing education. As a matter of fact, young Tom was letting his books take care of themselves. He was merely doing a little remembering from time to time, and his serious endeavors were lavished in winning the attentions of the prettiest girls in the college town. The only sport he favored was the old-fashioned and useless one—as far as newspapers were concerned—of fencing. Riding and fencing gave him his only exercise. His amusements were those of all prodigals, cards and drink, with other well-known things in between.

The four years at college cost his father a small fortune, but the older man consoled himself with the fine marks that young Tom secured in his studies, and so the bills were duly paid. Tom came home, hating his prospective ranch life like so many days of threatened prison. He also came home bringing his manservant, Bobbie, who had been through the whole college career with his master. But where college had been wasted on the master, it had not been lost upon the slave. Where Tom sat up to finish a bottle, Bobbie sat up to finish a book. Where Tom lounged in bed till noon, Bobbie was swinging through his paces in the college gymnasium, or on the athletic fields. It was little that Tom himself could do for his *alma mater*, but at least he could lend the services of Bobbie, and this was enough. Bobbie was the standard in the school of the sprinters. He was the iron man against whom the star linemen of the football team tried their strength. And it was a thing of beauty to see Bobbie, playing on the second eleven, melt through the center of the line and stop the plunging fullback before he had well started to plunge. They used to say of him that he had the speed of a cat and the power of a horse, but he was always as gentle as a man playing with children. If he tackled a runner, it was done with an almost apologetic firmness; in the boxing ring, if he blocked a hard swing with a stiff counter, he was busy with apologies at once. Someone told Farnsworth that he would have been detested for his profligacy in the university had it not been that one and all admitted that a man who could inspire such a servant with such devotion must have a good heart and a clean one. Bobbie was the shadow, it might be said, that set off young Tom and made him seem a highlight.

Then they came back to the ranch together, Bobbie placid, as always, with that infinite good nature that was his, like continual springtime, and Tom surly and sullen because he faced the long exile away from his boon companions and the city he loved. He would have gone mad with discontent had it not been that he met Deborah Kinkaid and lost his heart to her at once.

She was not at all of a type that one would have selected as an enchantress to enthrall young Tom. She was a small, wiry little person, with a head of the brightest red hair, a nose rather too short, blue, lively eyes, and a world of animation. When she met the young college man, she refused to be impressed by his dignity and sullen reserve.

"Anyone can look like a blunderbuss," said Deborah.

That remark was carried to Tom. He was furious and interested at once. He formed a contemptible scheme on the spot of making desperate love to Deborah until he had broken her heart. So he called on her at once. She showed him her pet horse and her pet duck. With mischievous eyes she sang ragtime to him across her piano. She sat under the huge cypress tree by the river, with her arms tucked behind her head, and confessed that she didn't know a thing about books now, didn't ever expect to, and hoped that she never would.

Tom went home with his head reeling. He could not sleep. Before morning he knew that he loved her, and he knew that she was below him. Moreover, he knew that on account of this girl he would have to stay in the West and endure people he despised and a country and climate made especially to be his bane. It was to forget Deborah that he had ridden into Daggett, played and lost his money, and then taken out his spite so shamefully on the big person of Bobbie.

II

No one carried to old Tom Farnsworth the tidings of how his son first beat Bobbie, but they could not help repeating how the big Negro had crushed Sam and Jud. Farnsworth made inquiry after that, learned the whole truth about the disgraceful fashion in which his son had behaved himself, and called young Tom before him—with thunder in his face.

"Tom," he said, "I'm ashamed of you and disgusted with you. And, by the eternal, unless you go this instant and beg the pardon of Bobbie, I swear I shall disinherit you. A Farnsworth to strike a servant . . . a Farnsworth! Thunderation, Tom, I see that you were created only to break my heart. This shame will never go out of the family."

Tom was brave enough. He dreaded nothing except the necessity of having to go to work. If he were disowned, he would have to labor with his hands. Rather than that, there was no humiliation through which he would not have passed. He went out, therefore, found Bobbie, and humbled himself before the Negro. But Bobbie would not hear him. It was not Master Tom who had struck him, he declared. It was simply a devil that had got into Master Tom for the moment, and which, he knew, would never come back again. But, no matter how much he said, he knew that young Tom would never forgive the servant, for the servant had been the means to this humiliation. He would far rather have faced the whipping again than to know that there was now a deep malice in the heart of young Tom Farnsworth.

Nor, in the meantime, were the results of that whipping ended. For, of course, the strange tale was carried straight to Deborah Kinkaid. She would not believe it at first, but, when the whole degrading fact was proved to her, she colored with shame and declared that, if she passed Tom Farnsworth again on the street, she would cut him dead. The very next day she did so straightway. To the amazement and the horror of young Tom, Deborah went by him with her head in the air, her eyes fixed on the enjoyment of some far-off prospect. He went home and lay all night in his bed, raging and tossing and twisting. First of all, he wanted to destroy the entire world and Deborah with it, and then he wanted to perish gloomily. Eventually he resolved to go East at once. He even leaped out of bed, dressed, and started to pack. But, after all, he decided that he would see Deborah again, even if his very heart had to bleed with the humiliation of bowing to her insult. For he could not go away before he had solved the mystery of why she was so hostile to him.

On the following night he went to see her. He slipped up behind the house and hesitated under the hedge for a long time. Young Jack Pattison was sitting on the porch, chatting with her, and the foolish laughter of the pair rattled and rang in his ears, tormenting him where he lay. Finally Pattison went away, and Tom got up to go to the girl before she entered the house. He must have a few words with her alone. If all did not turn out well, it must not be publicly known that he had so far debased himself that he had gone to cringe and crawl before this slip of a girl. For all the town of Daggett was repeating and relishing the story of how she had snubbed the rich man's son. He did not have a chance to see her in the dark of the porch, however, for young Jack Pattison had no sooner disappeared than she slipped into the house and ran up the stairs to her room. He saw the light flare in her window, and then he saw the shade pulled down, so that it became a dull rectangle, glowing. Then he decided that he must take one longer step in the adventure.

It was extremely rash. If he had been a thoughtful boy, he would never have done it, but Tom was not thoughtful. He followed the first impulse and went up the side of the house, climbing by means of the tree-like trunk and the sturdy branches of a great old climbing rose vine that had been planted when Mr. and Mrs. Kinkaid were married, and was, therefore, a year older than Deborah herself. It seemed a little wonderful to Tom, as he climbed, that creatures of one age should be so different—the vine, old and declining, Deborah in the very pink and flush of tender youth.

Now he sat on the ledge of her window, his heart thundering from the labor and the excitement of that climb. He tapped twice, cautiously. Suddenly it came to him with a shock that it would be a terrible thing if some other person should be in that room with the girl, if that other person—her mother, perhaps—should open the window and look down into his face. What could he do? He had no time to decide, for now the window was raised. The shade lifted, and there was Deborah herself just before him. He had been wondering how she would address him. He could never have guessed the words she chose.

She said simply: "Tom Farnsworth, you idiot! Tom, you *crazy* boy! What are you doing here?" And then, surprise and alarm both leaving her apparently, she dropped into a chair and burst into the heartiest laughter.

He studied her the while with a sort of gloomy disgust. She was not lovely, certainly. When she laughed, and one saw the alarming width of her mouth, she was not even pretty. Yet, while his reason dissected her and decided upon fault after fault she most unquestionably possessed, his instinct was every instant saying to him: *How delightful, how rapturously charming this creature is. Oh, oh, that she could be mine.*

"Why are you laughing, Deborah?"

"Because you look so perfectly undignified and unFarnsworthy on that windowsill. Come inside, Tom."

"Good heavens, Deborah, you don't think that I would do a thing that might compromise you."

"Hush," said the girl, with a careless gesture. "Do you think it's any better for me to have you seated in my window where everyone within a mile can see you?"

This suggestion made him tumble hastily into the room.

"Why did you come?" asked Deborah, very curious, and not a little excited, but still smiling, as she looked at the red fragments of bark that littered his clothes and the scratches on his face and his hands. A modern Romeo was Tom.

"Because I'm such a weak fool," said Tom, crimson with rage and shame. "Because . . ." He could not finish, but drew himself up and glowered down on her.

"Oh," said Deborah with a sudden change of tone. "I think I understand. You wanted to know why . . ."

"Yes."

"Because they told me that you flogged Bobbie."

"In the name of heaven," cried Tom, "what's Bobbie to you?"

"A fine fellow, I understand."

"A nigger . . . and a fine fellow?"

"Certainly! Why not? He's a human being, Tom."

"Deborah, if such a thing . . ."

"Well?"

He looked hopelessly at her. Every instant that she insulted and defied him made him pass through an agony of shame—and made him love her all the more violently.

"I'll say one thing!" she cried suddenly to him. "I was a nasty cat yesterday. I'm really sorry for it. I shouldn't have passed you in that way. I apologize, Tom."

It was not a great concession, but it quite melted Tom and made the way easier for him. "Deborah," he told her, "I've been

12

sick with it every moment of the time. Why the devil you did it, I can't make out. If you really mean that black rascal . . ."

"Why do you call him a rascal?"

"He's a nigger, isn't he?"

"Tom, everyone in Daggett respects him, and everyone is a little afraid of him."

"I wish his bones were bleaching in the rain!" Tom cried angrily. "But let's forget him. I've come here to talk about you and not about my valet."

She started to answer him with some heat, but then she changed her mind, after the fashion of one who feels that mere words are not tools sufficiently strong for the purpose at hand. "If you want to talk about me, I'm willing, of course," she said. "But you won't be silly, Tom?"

"You mean by that you hope I'll not be foolish enough to say that I love you. Is that it?"

"You have a nasty, sharp way of speaking, Tom."

"Frank people always hate frankness," he answered with equal testiness.

"Have you come to quarrel with me?" she asked, half angry and half smiling in spite of herself.

"I've come to make love to you," said Tom, "and I seem to be making a most awful mess of it."

"So you do . . . and yet . . ."

"Well?"

"I like you better this way than with the grand manner, Tom. I'd rather see you blush and grow angry than looking like the grand duke of something or other."

"Be serious for two seconds, Deborah."

"I am serious . . . more than you dream."

"I want to say two or three short words that have been said a good many times before. I want you to know that I love you, Deborah. Confound it, I've fought against it. I've told myself that, if I have to stay out here to court you, I'll lose you anyway . . . but, even if I win, it means that I'm condemned to spend the rest of my life in the West, because you'd never move to the East, I know."

"Never, Tom," she admitted, glad that he had passed from his declaration into something else that gave her a chance to take her breath. "Do you know I'm astonished?" she could not help adding.

"Nonsense! You've seen me hanging about you, mooning like a sick calf."

"I've seen you now and then, drifting near me and looking me over with a sort of contemplative amusement, as if you wondered what sort of a watch ticked behind the queer case." She said this without resentment.

"Good gad, Deborah, are you using me for your amusement?"

"I'm not a bit amused. I'm terribly excited."

"Then tell me what to expect, and I'll bother you no more."

"Even when you tell me you love me," she said with anger and curiosity commingled, "you speak more like a king than a suitor. I feel almost like crying . . . aye, aye, sir . . . like a sailor aboard a ship when the captain calls."

"Deborah, this is an infernally embarrassing position. I'm in a torment. Tell me yes or no, and then I'll go."

"I'd like to be so certain that I could answer it in that way, with a single word, and be sure that I'm right. Yesterday I was sure . . . but, when I heard how you'd treated Bobbie, I was convinced there was no man in the world so worthy of being hated. Today I'm beginning to doubt. Partly it's because I'm immensely flattered that you notice me . . . partly because I guess at all sorts of good things behind that cynical exterior of yours."

"You are a thousand times kind," he said coldly.

"There you are with your cynical touch again. Oh, Tom, confess frankly that you're carrying on this whole affair for a joke or a bet. Confess it, shake hands, and we'll part without malice."

A dull red burned up under his cheek, and, when he attempted to smile, his lips simply drew back in an ugly line. "That's your answer, then, Deborah?"

"It has to be. Let's be friends, Tom. Come to see me again. Let's grow to know one another."

"Every step I take toward you is an agony," he said. "The whole town of Daggett knows that you cut me, and the whole town will laugh and sneer when it sees me pursuing you."

"But you despise the whole town so much that you surely will not care a whit what it thinks of you."

He started at this and drew in his breath slowly, as though this were a new thought.

"It won't do, though," said the girl. "I think that I know how it is, Tom. You're one of those proud fellows who would sneer at the king of England to show your independence, but in your heart of hearts you care for the opinion of the smallest child and the poorest beggar on the street corner."

"Ridiculous!" Tom cried.

"I know I'm right."

He felt she had seen through him. He was partly relieved, partly amused, and in part he was very, very angry. It was just as if a strong man, in the midst of a passion of honest rage, should be tickled in the short ribs and forced to burst into laughter. What he wanted to do was to frown the opinion of Deborah into some other limbo, but what he did was to smile sheepishly upon her. "Confound it, Deborah," he said, "you turn me into a milk-and-water creature."

"Every minute," she said, "I see new things in you, Tom. Promise me that you'll do what I ask. We'll become friends. If the town of Daggett laughs at us, we'll laugh at the town of Daggett. And in the end we'll understand what's best to do. What's best right now is for you to go home . . . please. If someone should find you here, it would be mighty embarrassing."

"Shall I try to slip downstairs?"

"Dad is a wolf, when it comes to ears. You'd never get out that way. You'll have to go as you came."

He went to the window. "Deborah, I think that I shall go with hope."

"Of course you will."

She came up to him and took his hand, looking all the time into his eyes very earnestly, as though she were striving with all of her might to make out what might be going on inside his mind, guessing at the best, hoping for the best, but not quite sure. She seemed to Tom Farnsworth at that moment the loveliest and the best of women. He was so moved that he trembled—so shaken by her close scrutiny that he had to hide his face from her eyes by hurriedly raising her hand to his lips and then turning again to the window.

"Listen," she said as he sat poised for an instant on the window ledge, "I'll ride down to the river tomorrow, near the hill with the three willows on the top. I'll go in the middle of the afternoon when everyone else is sleeping. Will you be there, Tom?"

"A thousand soldiers couldn't keep me from being there. Good night, Deborah."

"Good night, Tom." She watched him swing into the darkness.

"Wild man . . . wild man," she whispered to herself, then closed the window, and drew back the shade once more.

III

As for Tom Farnsworth, he climbed down to the ground with a happy and reckless feeling growing in his heart. He had demeaned himself, of course, in going to her in this fashion, but dignity was one thing, and love was quite another, and they could not be near neighbors. She had despised him when he came; she had liked him well enough before he left. One more meeting might do much. He discovered that he no longer complained to himself because he was enchanted, as he had felt at first, without cause. Deborah became more and more one with his ideal of what a woman should be.

When he reached the earth, he was humming softly his content, and so, turning from the house, he saw a rudely outlined form in the darkness of the night, doubly black with the shadow of the house and the trees.

"What the devil . . . ?" began Tom.

"This is Jack Pattison," said the other quietly. "I wonder if I may have the privilege of a short chat with you, Farnsworth?"

Farnsworth followed him among the trees, bewildered, hot with shame, angry. "Now," he said, when at last they had reached a plot of open grass, "tell me what you want, Pattison?"

"An explanation."

"Really?"

"This night I have asked Deborah Kinkaid to be my wife. As I left the house and went down the road, I stopped a while behind the hedge to moon at her lighted window, like a fool. Then I saw something work up the side of the house. The window opened. A man clambered inside the room. I've waited here, Tom, to meet that man when he came down again. I suppose you understand what's on my mind?"

An impulse of good-natured openness formed in the brain of Tom. He wanted to make a clean breast of everything—of all the shame and dread of the public voice that had kept him from going to Deborah openly by day or night. He wanted to explain it all clearly, as from one friend to another, but he changed his mind at the last instant. He had not the moral courage to humiliate himself.

"I neither know nor care what's in your mind, Pattison," he said. "But what I wish to understand is . . . how do you dare to spy on me and then stop me to ask what's in my mind?"

"Is that your attitude?"

"That's my attitude."

"Then I have to tell you that you're an overbearing, egotistical ass, Farnsworth. You've made yourself despised and hated by everyone in the county. I'm glad to have this chance to tell you my own opinion."

"You have a polished tongue, Pattison."

"As for Deborah, trust me that I'll have a full explanation out of you."

"In what way, Pattison?"

"If I have to beat it out of you, I'll do it."

"Dear me," murmured Farnsworth. "You're a violent fellow, Pattison."

"Tom," cried the other, setting his grip on the breast of Farnsworth's coat, "you'll have to tell me everything I've asked, otherwise I'll go mad. I can't live and doubt Deborah."

The restraint with which Tom had held himself snapped. He struck off the hand of Pattison and leaped back. "Live or die and go to perdition for all of me!" he exclaimed. "Get out of my path, Pattison."

"Tom, this means a fight."

"As you please."

"Tom, I'm armed. For heaven's sake, be a man and a gentleman, and don't force us to do a murder here. I ask you for an explanation that you know I have a right to hear. Will you give it?"

"Not a syllable to any man on earth . . . by force."

"Then . . . God be on the right side!"

He jerked a hand for his hip pocket, but Farnsworth was much before him. He had already managed to shift his weapon to the deep pocket of his coat. He now dropped his hand upon it, found it lying already in line, and had merely to curl his finger around the trigger. Jack Pattison whirled around, throwing his revolver far into the brush, and fell on his face. The startling report of his own gun sobered and wakened Tom. He dropped instantly upon his knees beside the fallen man and turned him on his back. All that he could make out, in the dullness of the starlight, was the welling of blood from the very center of Pattison's forehead. Was he dead?

Tom stood up. Two birds, having been disturbed in their sleep by the roar of the gun beneath them, had soared a little distance into the air, but now they settled back to their roosting branch, with little sharp voices of complaint. The wind, tangling through some newly planted pine saplings, brought their freshness and purity of breath to Tom. Now he heard the outbreak of many voices from the Kinkaid house. A door slammed. Somebody ran noisily across the veranda.

"Who's there?" called Kinkaid. Then: "It came from yonder by the creek. Scatter, boys! Give a challenge as you go. If you meet anyone who won't speak, don't waste any time, but open up and . . ."

Tom Farnsworth was already out of the grove. He crossed the lawn beyond it like a sprinter. He dived through a hole in the old hedge. He twisted to the left and found his horse, waiting at the place where it had been left, but not the horse alone, for a mounted man, very tall and on a horse of great size, sat his saddle nearby, holding the reins of Tom's mount.

"Who's there?" gasped Tom, snatching out his gun as he ran.

"Bobbie!" called a guarded voice.

"Thank goodness . . . good boy." He flung himself into the saddle.

"What's happened, sir?"

It did not occur to Tom to keep back any secret from this man. "I've killed Jack Pattison."

"Lord, Lord!" groaned the Negro. "You're not sure, sir?"

"I shot him through the forehead . . . straight through the forehead, Bobbie. Can a man live after that?"

Another groan from Bobbie.

"What's to be done?"

"I'm thinkin' . . . I'm thinkin'."

"Best thing is to ride straight to the sheriff and give myself up. The sheriff would show me fair play."

"Master Tom, you're not very popular in Daggett just now. That was what brought me out after you tonight."

"What do you mean, Bobbie?"

"I mean that, when I saw you start for town, I guessed that there'd be trouble. So I came along."

"Start moving now. They're coming close."

The searchers from the house were beating through the garden, and now there was an outcry of horror. It could mean but one thing.

"They've found the dead body," said Tom. "Bobbie, this is my last minute as a free man. After this, I'm going to be a hound and run, and never stop running."

"Mister Tom, wait and listen to me. I have a way out of all this. You ride straight home. Don't go to the sheriff and tell him what you've done. Don't do that, but ride straight home. If you go to the sheriff, you can trust that a mob will go to the jail to lynch you. Everybody loved Jack Pattison. People will go wild when they learn what's happened to him. But you go straight home the way I tell you. When you get home, go right straight up to your bed and turn in."

"You want me to put my head quietly into the noose?" asked Tom.

"Mister Tom," said the Negro, "have I ever missed out on a promise I've made?"

"You haven't, Bobbie."

"Then just trust me this one time more to take you out of this trouble. I have a way all planned. Nobody will ever guess that you have a hand in what's happened tonight, unless Pattison wakes up and talks."

"I wish to goodness he would. If he'd talk again, I'd give them free leave to hang me. Bobbie, what can you do?"

"Just let it all to me, sir. I have a way in mind. But you have to go home first."

"Bobbie, God knows what devil got into me the other day when I struck you."

"I've forgotten what you mean, sir."

"You won't come with me, Bobbie?"

"No, sir."

"Good night, then, and good luck."

"Good night, sir."

Tom Farnsworth still hesitated for a little time, but now the noise from the Kinkaid house was growing more and more ugly. He could hear sounds from the stable behind the house, which was a very certain proof that they were saddling horses and making ready to pursue the murderer of poor Jack Pattison. Here was Bobbie, at whose side he somehow felt he should remain. But Bobbie was waving him away, and there the road stretched white and cool before him, twisting away into the pleasant darkness of the trees not far away. He let his long-legged bay mare drift softly through the silent dust that lay thick and light as feathers along the sides of the road. Presently, rounding the first turn and getting well out of the sight of the Kinkaid place, he gave the high-spirited creature her head, and she was away at once with a long, easy gallop. In the meantime, filled with a bitter concern, he wondered what could be in the mind of Bobbie.

"A nigger will show yellow sooner or later. Just give him time, and the bad streak will crop out," someone had said to him. He had never forgotten it. And he felt now an ugly premonition that Bobbie would use his knowledge of what had happened in order to get a full revenge for the beating he had received so lately. Indeed, he would be almost more than human, Farnsworth felt, if he did not make some use of that power now in his hands. He had merely to go to the men who were mustering at the Kinkaid house. A single word would send them thundering toward the Farnsworth house. So Tom drew up his horse and waited for a time to see what would happen, and in what direction the current of the pursuit would flow. He had not long to wait. There was a dim outbreak of yelling from the center of the town, which he had just left behind him. Then the voices began to recede rapidly, until he heard them no more, but only the hollow roar of hoofs, passing over a bridge. Tom gave this his own interpretation.

The cunning rascal, said Tom to himself, *he has told them that he saw the guilty man, and he has sent them on a wild-goose chase. He's a handy fellow to have, is Bobbie.*

IV

Bobbie had waited near the Kinkaid house with never a thought of treachery rising in his mind. His attitude toward his young master was a peculiar one. He did not love Tom. The blows that had been showered upon him lately had not been absolutely the first he had received. But, heretofore, Tom had been a little too much in awe of his gigantic servant to be free with punishment of a corporal nature. Yet he had taken Bobbie for granted from the first. They were almost exactly of an age. Bobbie was only a month or two older, but he had matured more quickly than the white boy, as Negroes almost always do. From the very first he had been little better than a slave to Tom. Never being without him, Tom had but a small value to place upon him. He heard other people make complimentary remarks about Bobbie, but he saw little reason for them. He accepted Bobbie as men accept pleasant weather with a sort of impersonal good nature.

Such was the attitude of Tom toward Bobbie, and of this attitude Bobbie was very well aware. For his own part he considered his master as a sort of limb of his own body. He could not separate himself from the thought of Tom Farnsworth. He reached the age of memory in the service of Tom. He had continued in it all his life. He could not possibly think of his own comfort and happiness first.

What he thought of, when Tom confessed that he had shot a man, was of his own grandfather when that dusky-faced, white-headed old man should hear the tidings that a Farnsworth had done a murder. What a passion of grief and of shame the old man would fall into, not because a Farnsworth could have committed a crime, but because his grandson could have allowed the crime to be committed. Such was the stern fashion in which he would take Bobbie to account. In the early days, when Tom was whipped by his father for stealing fruit or for any other of a thousand mischiefs, Bobbie was punished twice as severely by his grandfather, simply because he had not been able to invent the means of dissuading his young master from the crime.

So it was that on this night, as he heard Tom speaking, he saw the stern face of the aged Negro and shivered with apprehension. He would rather have faced a thousand whips, a thousand guns, than his irate grandfather in a bad temper.

"Son," the old man had said when the tidings had come of how Bobbie had been publicly flogged by Tom Farnsworth, "niggers is niggers these days. They's dirt. They ain't no more what they used to be. Oh, Bobbie, I ain't got the patience to talk none to you. Ah'm sick inside. You've made Master Tom disgrace himself before the whole town."

This was only a small sample of the sympathy poor Bobbie received upon this and other occasions. He was like one of those ministers who served a monarch in the days when "a king could do no wrong." The guilt of the ruler meant the death of the minister who had executed his decrees. So it was with Bobbie. And, as he learned from the lips of Tom himself that he had shot and killed young Pattison, all that Bobbie could do was say to himself: *I've got to find some way to bring him off. I can't face Granddad, if I fail Tom now.*

It was not, truly speaking, sheer love for the master, but it was that blind thing that sometimes keeps men marching and fighting and struggling to death, a thing divorced from love or even sympathy—the devotion to a cause. The Farnsworths were such a cause to Bobbie. Tom was part of the Farnsworths. So the servant marched resolutely ahead to take the risk upon his own head. He waited, first of all, until Tom was well out of sight down the thick gloom of the road. Then, sure that he could proceed without being recalled at a critical moment, he passed down the road slowly, keeping close to the fence, so that there would be the greater chance of his being seen from the garden. He was spotted almost at once.

"Hello!" someone sang out. "Who's there?"

Instead of answering, Bobbie ducked along the back of his horse and spurred away. This brought a shot, whistling above his head, and then a chorus of shouts: "I've seen him . . . a big man on a big horse . . . heading back through town."

Babel swelled up from the place. But already they had done much work and made many preparations. All that the people needed—they were saddling horses already—was such a stimulus as the explosion of that gun to make them leap into action. They rushed down the driveway from the stables and past Kinkaid's house. They spilled out into the street and spread out to keep from jostling, one against the other, until they saw in what direction they must next ride. So doing, they spotted the fugitive, moving swiftly down the street toward the very heart of the town. They raised a cry that would have done credit to a gang of Comanches newly riding on the warpath, with the blood appetite keen from long observance of peaceful ways. A score of men were almost instantly under way. For there were the men from Kinkaid's place plus neighbors who had heard the shot and happened to have horses standing ready—for it was not very late in the night. Still others rushed to stables and tossed saddles on their mounts when they heard that wild and long-drawn yell from many throats, serving as a signal to tell every man in town that the quarry was running, and that he was in full flight. So they stormed in pursuit of the hunted, eager to come up and lend a hand to the good work. And work it was, before the morning dawned upon them.

Bobbie went through the center of Daggett, twisting at every corner. He did not race his horse. In fact, the animal would not stand racing. It was a sturdily built roan, able to carry the two hundred and forty pounds Bobbie weighed in his clothes. No spindle-legged sprinter of a horse could be expected to handle Bobbie's weight, with the added pounds of a saddle that had to be made extra large and strong for the same reason. The result was that Bobbie had to be mounted on a thirteen-hundred-pound giant with sturdy ways and only an immense amount of endurance to recommend him. He had the two points that mean toughness, as a rule. The one was his roan coloring; the other was his Roman nose. The roan could strike a long canter and keep to it through most of a day, even with the burden of Bobbie on his back. It was at this pace—or at only just a little more—that Bobbie went through the town. Every time he turned a corner, he could do it without drawing rein. Every time the pursuit foamed around the corner behind him, it swung wide. Racing horses crashed against one another. Men lost their tempers and blamed one another heartily. But they gained very little ground on Bobbie and the roan.

Then they drew out of Daggett. On the outskirts someone yelled: "What's Bobbie done?" It was a boy's piping voice that could be heard half a mile away.

"It's Bobbie!" ran another voice through the posse. And they repeated it with an oath: "It's Bobbie! There'll be dead men among us before we ever get that coon. If he's gone bad, he'll turn out a plumb lion."

They straightway settled down for a long hunt. Those who happened to be better mounted than the rest did not press rashly forward in the hunt—for every man of them had seen Bobbie take a Colt in either hand and roll two tin cans in differing directions, kicking them along with sprays of dust, as the slugs spat into the ground just in the rear. They had seen him do tricks with a rifle, also. They had watched him box. For every man could well recall that historic occasion when the great black, who was battling upward among the ranks of the country's heavyweights, had paused at Daggett to astonish the natives with his prowess. Bobbie had taken a bet and gone in against him. They had fought mightily, and young Bobbie had at last struck that Negro beneath the heart and then beneath the jaw with all his force, sending him to the hospital to recover. They knew all of these things about Bobbie. If he could do so many things in sport, they could not help wondering what he would be able to do when he was fighting desperately for his life. At least they were unwilling to crowd him. When the daylight came, they would be prepared to open up their guns on him and bring him back to them. So they pushed steadily on, but made no endeavor to run him down suddenly. They wanted, if possible, a peaceful surrender, not a butchery. But that peaceful surrender, they knew, would mean a lynching for Bobbie when he was brought back to Daggett, for, as they rushed out of the town, the word had been whispered among them that poor Jack Pattison was breathing, indeed, but fast dying—that he could not possibly live until the morning light began the new day.

They stormed along behind Bobbie out of Daggett, down the dry course of the Pickett River, and to the rise of hills that had been dignified by the title of the Daggett Mountains. They might have served for mountains in Wales or Scotland, but here, where Nature worked with a generous and a more hastily liberal hand, they were no more than hills. Into these they pushed Bobbie, who still fled fast before them.

Just before dawn he reached Milton Harrwitz's place. He spurred with all the might of his roan down the slope, leading to the ranch in the hollow. In the field he roped a muscular five-year-old gray gelding, pitched a saddle onto its back, and rode off like mad again, with the bullets beginning to whistle around his

MAX BRAND

head. As he rode, he twisted on the back of the gelding and managed to pass the girths beneath the belly on the galloping horse, and so to cinch them up—a feat truly close to the miraculous. But in ten minutes all was settled, the gray had not lost ground, and the moment Bobbie settled down to the work of seriously jockeying him, the gray began to make a gap between the big Negro and the pursuers.

Mischief, however, had been born by that maneuver. Bobbie had forgotten something of the most vital importance, something that no one west of the Mississippi is allowed to neglect. There may be reasons why one man may kill another man; there are even known occasions when it is a desirable and highly honorable affair. But there is never any occasion when the theft of a horse can be overlooked. If the posse worked honestly to get at Bobbie before, it now worked in feverish earnest.

He fled all that day and into the next night. Then he was headed. The telegraph had worked against him in a round-about fashion. The wire had gone triangling clear up to Denver and then back again to Kiever City. From Kiever two score men and youngsters, who had nothing better to do, spread across the hills to find the Negro. They went in groups of three to five, well armed. Some of them had dogs—big hounds were popular in that district, being crosses of the mastiff and the greyhound breed. They had the burly shoulders and the fighting jaws and wills of the former breed and something of the speed and the endurance of the latter. Four men and four dogs fell across the trail of Bobbie. It is known through all the district, five hundred miles in any direction, that the men of Kiever City are like their dogs, strong and lean and swift and hard fighters. And their horses are like the men and the dogs. Yet Bobbie gave them the slip. As the four plunged on through the gray of the dawn, they heard one voice, of the four that bayed before them, grow silent. Then another ended, and then a third. The fourth dog raised a wail, and they rode swiftly up on him. They passed one huge brute with its throat slashed open, then another, and at the third dead body they found the fourth dog, the sole survivor, standing to mourn its mate. How Bobbie had done it they could not tell, but he must have found a way of swinging back in the saddle and meeting the leap of each hound with the slash of his long-bladed hunting knife.

They spread the tidings quickly to their companions in the hills. Such news travels without the aid of a telegraph wire. They learned that Bobbie was a dangerous man, indeed. The very next night he proved it. He had been flying for three days now, without rest or sleep. He had stolen and changed horses twice more on his way. But still the pursuers rose up out of the ground before him and clung in his rear, for the men of Kiever City and the Kiever Mountains do not give up a trail easily. Apparently he saw that straightway flight could not save him. He doubled straight down a narrow cañon, fell upon a party of three who were riding hotly after him, and went cleanly through them. He shot the first man off his horse, driving the bullet through the fellow's right thigh. Then he dropped his revolver and caught at the other two with his bare hands. He emptied two saddles with two gestures and left two writhing, stricken men on the ground behind him, as he cantered away, leading their horses. To those horses he changed. It was two long hours before they could spread the tidings of how he had broken through their ring, and by that time Bobbie was twenty miles, or thereabouts, away. He had this advantage: he had dodged all pursuit and could now hide and rest himself and his horse. He had this disadvantage: the men of Kiever City and the Kiever Mountains now felt it their duty and incumbent upon their honor to hunt Bobbie to the death.

V

On the second morning after the melodramatic flight of Bobbie, his young master, Tom Farnsworth, rode down the countryside and found the ranch of Milton Harrwitz. Harrwitz was a Russian who had lived on the Steppes in his youth, and he had learned how to ride and raise cattle from the Tartars when he was a boy, having been stolen and carried away by a group of wild nomadic marauders. When he was twenty, he was a chief, because his long legs could cling to a horse and his hands could shoot a rifle with great precision. At twenty-five he met a romantic American girl, won her heart by his wild, strange face and his horsemanship, married her, and came to the States. There he broke her heart, spent her money, left her dying behind him, and went West. The cow range was nearer to his heart and his liking than anything he had seen since Siberia. He took the remnant of his wife's money, bought a small herd, and ever since that time had slowly prospered. Now he was worth some hundreds of thousands. He was still a barbarian, but he had lived so long in the community that his neighbors were willing to overlook many of his faults. Like most Russians he was a good neighbor, true to those who trusted him, liberal with money to a friend, and, above all, an implacable enemy to those who excited his wrath. All of these qualities were highly admirable in the eyes of the men of the cow country. They were rather awe-stricken by the black squalor in which Harrwitz lived, by his swarthy, greasy skin, his bright eyes, and his smile like the hungry grin of a beast. But he had been a hero when the last forest fire swept the hills, and his other qualities had been proven. No one in the county would be more readily listened to.

Young Tom Farnsworth approached this formidable Russian with a good deal of trepidation and a good deal of disgust. He arrived just before noon, and he found a few Mexican cowpunchers sitting about the door of the adobe hut where Harrwitz lived. They rolled their cigarettes and jerked a thumb to indicate that Harrwitz was inside. Tom Farnsworth entered and was staggered by the incredible filth of the room that was kitchen, living room, and dining room. It was odd that the Mexicans would accept such surroundings, but it was known that only the lowest of the low refugees from justice, brutes of a thousand crimes, came to Harrwitz who asked from them only hard work, and who gave them high pay and no questions. Tom pushed his way to an inner door, thrust it open, and found himself in a small, stuffy compartment, the one window of which was closed tight, so that the temperature of the air in the room had raised to almost blood heat. There was an old-fashioned four-poster bed, so big that it occupied nearly two thirds of the floor space of the dirty room. A few rags of faded cloth hung from the upper frame, all that remained of its canopy. The paint and the varnish had peeled away in the heat and had been worn away by the scraping of spurred heels and the scratching of matches. Harrwitz lay prone on the bed, face downward, his face muffled in a mass of ragged old quilts whose colors were long since covered with dirt. He lay like a dead man, and Tom Farnsworth half suspected he had been murdered, until he saw the back of the man stir with deep, regular breathing. He was sleeping, exhausted. For Harrwitz had been up for three days and three nights, caring for sick cows. He was worn out by his work, but he had saved lives, which meant dollars, and now he slept the sleep of deep contentment. He was satisfied.

He wakened with a shudder of anguish and turned to Tom Farnsworth a haggard face, unshaven for a fortnight, with the result that long, black bristles thrust out sparsely here and there over his leathery countenance. He staggered to a corner of the room, lifting up a dipper of lukewarm water from a bucket, swallowed some, and poured the rest over the back of his neck and head, letting it drip and soak into his shirt and underclothes of thick red flannel. A shake of his head finished the work of clearing his senses, and he asked Tom what brought him here.

"My man, Bobbie," said young Tom, "stole a horse of yours. I've come to pay you for him."

"Ah?" said Harrwitz, and his face brightened at the mention of that welcome word, *pay*. He led the way to the outside. He did not make the Mexicans get up to give them stools, but he dragged out two staggering boxes in which groceries had been recently delivered.

"That gray horse," said Harrwitz, "that gray horse was one of the chosen and the choice ones, Mister Farnsworth. You might say I knowed the insides of the mind of that there colt."

"No doubt," said Farnsworth, too disgusted with the face and the smell of the man to prolong the conversation. "No doubt that the horse was an intimate friend, and that you have felt his loss very keenly. Perhaps he will one of these days be returned to you. In the meantime I wish to pay you for his full value, even for the loss of his companionship."

One would have said that Harrwitz accepted this sarcasm in all seriousness, for he began to nod, screwing the center of his mouth up and the sides of it down, while he turned out the palms of his hands with one of those eloquent gestures of his race. "But, Mister Farnsworth . . ."

"Well?" asked Tom sharply. "Put the price high, if you wish to. Anything in reason, Harrwitz, or even a little more than reason."

"What you want is that I don't catch him for a thief."

"That's it," said Tom.

"Ah, ah," said Harrwitz, sucking in his breath. "But what good is that? If they catch him, they hang him for killing Pattison . . . no?"

"Pattison isn't dead," said Tom. "He's still living. He's delirious. Has brain fever or something like that. May never speak sense again . . . chances are that he'll die . . . but, if he doesn't die"—Tom ended somewhat dubiously—"he'll live to clear Bobbie, perhaps . . ."

Harrwitz grinned. "You make it funny, Mister Farnsworth. Why don't you laugh?" He looked up at Tom, boring him with little keen eyes that, it was said, had looked their way into many an important secret.

Tom trembled momentarily at his own secret. Yet, as he reflected, Bobbie had so perfectly covered the trail by taking all suspicion on his own shoulders that Tom presently regained his self-possession. He began to argue his point, even with this low fellow. "Consider this, Harrwitz . . . they were milling about in the place of Kinkaid. Someone saw Bobbie ride along the hedge. They shouted at him. He probably looked across the hedge and saw twenty men, walking about in the grounds. He may have become frightened. Sometimes Negroes get shabby justice from a crowd. Instead of waiting and answering, he rode away. Then the whole crowd of 'em took after him. He lost his head and rode like a mad man through Daggett. He knew he was innocent, perhaps, but he also knew that they were after him. He rode for his life. Reached your place, found his horse failing, stole another, and rode on. Then he may have reflected that he was a criminal, after stealing a horse, so the poor simple fellow has kept on running and fighting in order to get clear. If I can settle this horse theft, perhaps we can bring Bobbie back to us, while we locate the real criminal. What had Bobbie against Pattison? What would he gain by killing such a man?" His voice rose at the end.

Harrwitz considered this harangue soberly. "He stole a horse," he said at last. "He stole my horse. *He'll* have to pay for it . . . not you. I want *his* money, not yours." That was his way of seeing justice done.

"What was the price of the gray horse?" asked Tom, seeing that he could not talk of abstractions to a man with so much malice in him.

"Oh, maybe two hundred dollars."

That was about double a fair price, as Tom knew, but he pulled out his wallet at once. "I have two hundred dollars for you, Harrwitz."

"Is it Bobbie's money?"

"Yes, because I'm using it for him."

"Let him come to pay it to me then. I want to talk with him." As he spoke, he fondled the butt of his Colt absently.

"I'll make it a shade more, Harrwitz, considering how much the gray meant to you. I'll make it two hundred and fifty dollars."

"Right quick . . . spot cash?"

"Yes."

Harrwitz ran the red tip of his tongue across his greasy lips. "I guess that I don't want your money. It ain't right," he said finally.

"Three hundred dollars, Harrwitz!"

The Russian stared at him. Then he pointed down the valley. "You see by the river bottom a hundred acres . . . that's worth two hundred an acre. Well, Mister Farnsworth, if you give me another hundred acres just like that for the gray horse, I take the horse and leave you the acres."

"What *do* you want?"

"My rights," said the other.

Tom, meeting the glittering eyes for another moment, saw that there was nothing but wasted time in such a conversation.

He rode back to Daggett and through Daggett to his father's ranch which he reached, with a staggering horse, at sunset. The old grandfather of Bobbie came out of the stable to take his young master's horse. Age had withered him without bowing his body. The lids were puckered around eyes that were still intelligent and bright. His step was short, but light and steady.

"Uncle," said Tom, "has any news come in?"

"There ain't goin' to be no news, Master Tom," said the Negro. "There ain't goin' to be no news till we hear that they've caught Bobbie and strung him up to a tree."

"That's a terrible thing to say."

"Books ain't for niggers," said the old dark man. "Bobbie read too much. He could talk too much. And the same bad streak in his daddy was a streak in Bobbie. I know."

"But suppose that he didn't do the shooting?"

The old Negro started at this suggestion. It seemed to bewilder more than please him. "If he didn't do nothin', but run just the same, then he's a fool. And a fool is pretty near as bad as a murderer, Master Tom."

Young Farnsworth went to the house. He had barely entered when his father came hurrying out to him with a note in his hand.

"Here's a letter from town . . . it's from old Pattison. He's sent for you, Tom. His boy isn't any better, but his head has cleared up some, and he's asking for you."

VI

It was a thunderstroke for Tom. At first he put the simplest possible interpretation upon it, which was that young Pattison, recovering his senses, had denounced Tom as his destroyer and called upon his father to avenge him. Pattison, Sr. had sent for him and would have the sheriff waiting when he came. To face a murder charge, as he now saw, would be a simple thing compared with the shame of having to confess that he had allowed his manservant to take the deadly burden of the suspicion on his shoulders and draw the vengeance of the law after him. He hesitated for ten seconds, revolving that thought in his brain. Then he determined that he would have to face Pattison, no matter what the consequences. If he did not come, and they indeed suspected him, they could apprehend him in his home. The only question in his mind was whether he would flee to the mountains and embrace outlawry, or else go to Pattison and meet whatever lay in wait for him there. To give up all that was pleasant to him in life for the sake of a roving existence in the wilderness was more than he was prepared to do. Hanging itself would not be much more bitter. So at length he had a fresh horse saddled, changed to fresh clothes after a bath, and in the dark of the evening, with his head high and the sweet aroma of an Egyptian cigarette in his nostrils, he rode for the Pattison house in Daggett.

It was the most gloomy and mysterious time of the evening. Across the fields a low-flying hoot owl pursued him, unseen, but with melancholy voice rolling about him now and again. He passed an old buggy, wheeling softly through the dust, with all the figures in it turned to shapeless blotches in the night. A man's voice and a girl's were singing and, as he passed into the acrid dust cloud on their back trail, the song floated dimly behind him. It stopped. The wheels of the rig rattled over a bump, then the horse pounded with hollow tread over a distant wooden culvert, and Tom was left alone on his path again. He went on with an empty heart, for that happy singing suggested to him such a picture of innocent contentment that his own crime seemed blacker than before. Being so sad of mind, he hurried on his way more quickly than ever. He reached Daggett and passed to the house of Pattison.

Old Pattison met him in the hall. "My dear Tom," he said, "I had no idea that you and my boy were such good friends. But he's been asking for no one else for hours."

"Poor Jack," murmured the hypocrite. "How is he now?"

"Very low . . . very low, indeed. God alone knows what will come to him. We pray, Tom, but we fear that the worst is about to come to us. The bullet passed through his head."

"I'll go in to him," said Tom hastily, and, leaving the father behind him, he went to Jack Pattison.

He found Jack's face very pale, looking thinner and older by many years. The youngster's eyes were almost closed, and they were surrounded by great blue-black circles. Someone in white rose from a chair beside the bed. Tom had never seen her before, but the nurse apparently knew who he was. She leaned over the sufferer and took his arm gently.

"Mister Pattison, here is Mister Farnsworth to see you. You may talk with him if you will promise not to stir so much as a hand . . . and not to speak above a whisper." She stepped back, turning to Tom. "You may have one minute with him," she told

Tom, and, moving toward the wall of the room, she began to study the face of her watch, counting off the quick seconds.

"It's I, Jack," whispered Tom.

"Tom," murmured the wounded man faintly. "I wanted to tell you that I'll not let a soul know who did this thing. I've closed the door on it. In exchange for that promise I want you to tell me the thing you know I want to learn."

"I'll tell you frankly, Jack," said the other, immensely relieved, and now beginning to pity the wounded man. "I merely forced my way into her room the other night . . . or, rather, to her window, because I had to try to reinstate myself. She had cut me dead only a little while before, as you know. I was desperate, Jack, and I didn't dare to face her before other people, because I was fairly sure that she would cut me again."

There was a sigh of happiness from Jack. "I've been lying here in a fire of doubt," he confessed. "But now I know that you've told me the truth, and I think that it gives me almost enough strength to cure me. Tom . . . "

"There is no more time," said the nurse, stepping up to the bedside. "The doctor's order was very strict."

Tom stepped away. He could have sung with happiness as he reached the door, and beyond it, in the hall, he talked for a moment with the father, who had been waiting anxiously for him. It was not hard to explain the interview.

"Sick people get queer longings," said Tom to the father. "When I was a youngster, I had scarlet fever. I remember that the thing that haunted me was the desire for raw roast beef. Queer, eh? That's the way with Jack. He happened to fix his mind on me. And he kept it fixed for so long a time that he finally had to see me."

The nurse came out from the sick room with an excited, happy face.

"He's asleep," she said. "Send the message to the doctor, Mister Pattison. The moment Mister Farnsworth left the room he fell asleep. His pulse is steady . . . his nerves are better . . . his temperature is falling. Mister Farnsworth must have brought him good news."

Pattison, frantic with happiness, hastened off to find the doctor, and Tom rode back to call on the lady of his heart. He was brought into the library of the old house and sat down to wait for her, feeling decidedly stiff and uncomfortable. The room was furnished after the pattern of thirty years before. The chairs were covered in glossy horsehair. There was a couch upholstered in the same material with a little round cushion on it. The carpet was blue, strewn with great roses. Gothic bookcases went around the walls. Behind the glass of the doors stood long sets whose glimmering backs betrayed that the volumes had never been frayed and worn by handling. Some of the doors, in fact, were closed tighter than with a lock because, being undisturbed for months at a time, the varnish had sweated and held like a stout glue. He had seen those same familiar faces in every library of the ranch houses of any pretension in the county.

The desk of Mr. Kinkaid was in a corner of the room with a swivel chair before it. It had a great broad blotter on the top, a rack of pens at hand, and a calendar in sight. But it was well known that Mr. Kinkaid never sat here. He carried his business in his head. He could tell you at any time just how many cows and calves were on his ranches, and what condition they were in, and how the market stood, and how the grass was looking in every corner of his places. His office was his saddle, and his office force consisted of his own strong, swiftly moving, accurate brain.

Such was the man, and such was the room in which Tom presently slid off the glossy seat of a chair and came to his feet, for Deborah stood in the doorway. She went straight to him, but, instead of shaking hands, she dropped into a chair and faced him, beckoning him to take an opposite seat.

"What have you come to tell me, Tom?"

"That Pattison is immensely better. I went to see him tonight."

"Really?"

"Why not? I've always liked Jack."

"Of course," murmured Deborah. "Everyone has always liked poor Jack."

"He sent for me, as a matter of fact."

"I didn't know you were such friends."

"Just a sick man's freak. I talked to him one minute, about nothing. Then I came away . . . but, before I left the house, we learned from the nurse that he had fallen in a sound, even sleep, and that his nerves were quieter . . . that he would awaken much stronger and better able to make a fight for his life."

"Good! Good! I'm so happy . . . so very happy, Tom! And now, what's the news of Bobbie?"

"The last we heard he was doubling into the Kiever Mountains. The Kiever men are wild over the hunt."

"And they're terrible people, aren't they?"

"They're supposed to be, but I've an idea that Bobbie will prove a match for them."

"Suppose he doesn't?"

"Well, a man has to take his punishment when he commits a crime like murder, Deborah."

She stirred in her chair, as though the thought pricked her to the quick. And Tom, staring hard at her, saw that her pallor had given way to a bright flush of excitement.

"Perhaps you're right, Tom. Murder will out, as people say."

She said this with a certain dryness of tone, such as people use when they have in mind a double innuendo.

"What do you mean by that remark, Deborah?" he asked her with a sick suspicion beginning to grow in him.

"I'll be franker with you than you've been with me. Tom, you were sent for by poor Jack because he was tormented with worries about me. He'd seen you climb up through the window of my room."

Young Farnsworth grew bolt erect in his chair. Something was born in him then that he had never felt in himself before in all his life. It was a consummate desire to destroy with his hands. He had not even felt it when he faced Jack the other night. On that occasion he had fought suddenly and shot to kill, but it had been because his back was against the wall. Now, as the girl struck at him, by sudden surprise, his first impulse was a red rage and a passionate desire to take her with his hands . . . He controlled that impulse, marveling at himself, and watched the emotion die away in him, as an echo dies far down a canyon. Nevertheless, he felt that hot rush of blood to the head might come again, and, if it were any stronger, he would not be able to master himself. It filled him with awe. It also filled him with pride to know that he had in himself the sway of passions greater than his ability to control them. If he had made this discovery of new powers in himself, why might there not be other discoveries in the future? Anything became possible. He became a new country to himself. This was the attitude of Tom, and, as he faced the girl, he realized that she no longer meant to him what she had meant before. She had become a danger and a threat to him. Affection for her began to die at the roots of his heart.

"He wanted to know what brought you there," continued the steady voice of Deborah. "And he offered in exchange to keep it secret that you were the man, Tom, who shot him down." She faced him steadily.

He could not remain seated in the face of this attack. But, as he came to his feet, flaring at her, his cleared eyes looked through and through her, discerned all the glamour of her beauty fading from her, found her small, plain face common, and he marveled beyond words that he could ever have wasted any time on her. He almost thanked God that this tragic story had come about, if it could at least waken him to the truth about the lady of his heart. He wanted to laugh. Then he was disgusted by his own lack of taste. Last of all the hot anger that had gripped him just before swept over him again. She was assailing him, and he had to defend himself—with words.

"Deborah," he said at last, "I'll tell you the facts."

He considered another moment, made up his mind definitely that it was better to confess than to arouse her suspicions by lying. Still, it was strange that she could have seen their meeting, since her shade had been drawn, as he was sure it had been. Perhaps she had spied down at him through a crack at the side.

"I shot Jack," he said bluntly, "but it was because he forced the fight on me."

She started in her place and drew in a gasping breath.

"You didn't see it, after all?" he asked sharply.

"I only guessed," she confessed.

The hot wave came darkly upon his eyes once more. He had to clench his hands for a moment before his vision and his self-control returned.

"You are very angry?" said the girl curiously.

"You've made a fool of me."

"A fool?"

"You've set this little trap for me."

"Tom, I had not even a suspicion about you when you came this evening. But, while you were here, it jumped into my mind. I can't tell what had put it there. And still I can't believe it. You . . . you shot poor Jack Pattison?"

"In a fair fight!" cried Tom.

She waved her hand. "Frankly I don't believe it."

"Do you accuse me of lying, Deborah? Is that what your friendship means?"

"I'm afraid that my friendship is dead."

"I swear to you, Deborah, that he started a hand for his gun before I stirred for mine."

"The real point of the matter," she said, skipping over what she was certain was the crux of the story and the evidence, "is that you shot Pattison and then allowed another man to take the blame for that work."

"How could I keep Bobbie from making a fool of himself?"

"Do you want me to tell you what I think? But, no, I won't tell you that. It's too easy to speak too much about such things. I won't tell you. Only . . . you mustn't be surprised if men who hear this grow a little angry with you."

"That infernal fool will be the destruction of me," said Tom Farnsworth gloomily. "Why didn't I tell him to go to the devil? As a matter of fact, Deborah, I knew nothing about what Bobbie intended. When he ran away and drew the rest of 'em after him, I was the most surprised man in Daggett. It was simply useless, foolish devotion on the part of Bobbie."

"I see," said Deborah, and smiled coldly at him.

He had been telling the truth on the whole. Now he flushed with rage. "You don't believe me?"

She rose and went to the door. "I suppose," she said, studying her words carefully, "that this is the last time I shall have an opportunity of talking with you, Tom."

"What does that mean?" Then panic succeeded his anger. "Good God, Deborah, it doesn't mean that you'd deliberately tell what . . ."

"Go on."

"Tell what I've spoken to you in absolute confidence."

"When I'd wrung it out of you by a trick, Tom? No, I don't think that I'd be violating a confidence." Her eyes were impudent.

"You really mean, then, that you'll go to the sheriff with this rotten story? Don't you see that it'll make trouble for me, but that I can't be harmed in the end? Jack himself would testify for me."

"Poor, honest Jack. If anything happens to him . . ." She controlled herself sternly. "Listen to me, Tom," she said, "what I firmly believe about you is what I'm going to tell you now. When I've told my story, I'm sure that it's what every other man and woman in Daggett will believe. You tried to kill poor Jack Pattison when he met you after you'd climbed down from my window."

"What will become of your reputation when you tell a story that has in it details such as this?"

"I thank God," said the girl quietly, "that my reputation is stronger than rock. I say that you shot Jack . . . probably through treachery, because he was known to be as good a shot as you are a bad one."

"Good Lord!"

"Be patient till I'm ended, please. You shot Jack . . . you let your poor Negro take the blame on his shoulders . . . you let him run the danger of being shot as a murderer and a horse thief, and all the while you dared to pose as an innocent man in Daggett. It's a black, black story, Tom. And I tell you plainly this much . . . if Bobbie is not brought back to safety . . . poor faithful fool . . . I'll tell."

"Suppose he's killed before I can reach him?"

"If that happens, it isn't your fault. Oh, Tom, even if you will make one great effort to save that poor black man, I swear that my lips are sealed forever. I'll never tell what I guess and what I know through your own confession."

VII

How often one hears the remark concerning a patiently working horse: "If only it knew its strength." The same thing is rarely said about a man, for the picture that fills the eye is of the great bulk of twelve or fifteen hundredweight of bone and muscle turned in revolt, smashing the wagon it pulls and the harness that attempts to control it, killing the driver with the blow of a hoof, or destroying the rider with a crunch of teeth stronger than a tiger's. If a man is wakened to lawlessness, his power is yet more terrible. He banishes with a gesture of the mind the load of duty at which he has been tugging. He annihilates the law by merely denying it. He trebles his strength by freedom that is absolute. He adds to the strength of a man the strength of a wild beast by casting himself loose from society.

Such was the case of Bobbie. He had started on this affair as upon a most perilous adventure to which he was compelled only because he loved his master far more than he loved himself. For the sake of his young master he had ridden through the midst of perils on that first night and through the days that followed. But now he was beginning to forget that he had started out for the sake of another person. The game was worthwhile on its own account. He could not recall another period in his life when he had enjoyed a tithe of this happiness. He was playing a game of chess. Upon his side there were only two pieces—himself and his horse. On the other side was a filled board, and only by the most complicated maneuvers could he escape them. He could not have survived for a single day had he not been among the Kiever Mountains, for they were created especially, so it seemed, to give a fugitive a chance to dodge away from his pursuers. The Kiever Mountains run from end to end through a distance of seventy miles, curving from northeast to southwest. The plateau in which they have footing is two thousand feet above the level of the sea. The loftiest peaks of the Kiever range are not more than three thousand feet above this point. The king of them all is a scant fifty feet short of a mile in elevation. In a word, they are small mountains for a country such as the great mountain desert, but they use every inch of their size for the greatest possible roughness. They are hewed across and up and down by great ravines, so that a picture from above would make the range look like a butcher's chopping block. There are not many trees, but there is sagebrush scattered here and there and a quantity of other small growths. Now and again, moreover, where there is water in a lowland or in a deep valley, one comes upon an almost tropical forest, for the soil is everywhere rich when it is deep enough to receive roots. This is not frequent in the range, however, and the majority of the upper slopes and of the mountain heads consist of junk heaps of stones and boulders and long slides of rock, still wearing the polish that was placed upon it during the glacial age. In this region of a myriad of rocks and a million hollows and gorges Bobbie found that he could hide so readily that it was even extremely difficult to find his own way. For two days he wandered in despair, appalled by the white-hot heat of the days, the cold of the nights, the lack of water, the scant provender that soon had the ribs of his horse thrusting out, and the difficulty of game. There were rabbits, of course, for there are rabbits everywhere, but there was little else. And the stomach of Bobbie revolted at his very second day of fare consisting of only one article of diet.

His first exploit was undertaken purely with the view to recruiting his own larder. He had no higher motive, nor did he have the slightest desire to break away from the Kiever Mountains for, when he climbed to the central peaks, he could see out onto the wide sweep of desert and level plain beyond. In this covert he might prolong the game for some time. In yonder open he would receive a mate in the form of an ounce of lead planted skillfully among his ribs. So he contented himself with making himself in the first place master of his position.

This he did by spending some hours on the top of Old Kiever itself, as the highest of the peaks was called. From this point of vantage he could make out clearly enough and jot down in his mind the various landmarks up and down the length of the range. Keeping these firmly in his recollection, he had only to consult his mental notebook in order to tell himself where he was at any point in his later wanderings. He had reached this point in understanding of his environment when the delicately nurtured stomach of Bobbie demanded a change of diet and forced him out of his inner retreats, toward which the hunting parties had been laboring on both days with the dogs to lead them.

He stole down to the foot of the eastern mountains, and on the shores of a little pool he found a newly arrived party of a dozen honest citizens who had come out to join in this rare sport and to avenge the honor and fair fame of the town of Kiever. This was not a haphazard crew. Among them was the ex-sheriff, who secretly hoped to restore himself to the good graces of the voters in the county by rounding up the fugitive who had hitherto baffled both the regular and the irregular forces of the law in Kiever County. Accordingly this well-equipped and managed party went to sleep at the watering place only after all the horses had been well hobbled and a guard had been posted—the wariest and sharpest-eared member of the entire group, who could not conceivably doze.

Bobbie, slipping down among the shadows of the trees, took note. The watcher had placed himself on the top of a stone that sat on the edge of the pool. His back was to the water, since he was safe from attack in that direction. His eyes restlessly turned up and down the shore, sweeping over the sleepers and their effects. And across his knees, ready for instant action, lay a rifle with fifteen shots tucked into the magazine. When Bobbie had observed these things, he made his plan at once, skirted around to the other side of the pool, took off his clothes, and slid down into the warm water, a deep shadow among shadows. One who had learned to high dive from a springboard and enter the swimming pool with such oiled smoothness that hardly a ripple ran out around the point at which he entered certainly found no trouble in entering this pool without a sound. He melted into the black water and disappeared at once. For a moment he was out of view. Then a little ripple began to travel across the tiny lake. In the center of the ripple the nose of Bobbie projected to the air. Beneath the ripple his powerful arms and legs moved in a soft rhythm, sending him in slow pulses across to the other shore.

When he was near the spot, he sank deeper in the water, turned, dived, and came up directly behind the watcher on the stone. There was no struggle. Bobbie rose to his knees. He picked up the guard's own coat which lay neatly folded on the ground. That coat he flung like a net over the head of the unfortunate.

Then, when he had stopped the noise of cries, he stopped the noise of struggles also, by discreetly tapping the padded head of the sentinel with a rock. Thus put to sleep, the watcher was laid behind the rock on which he had been sitting, and Bobbie proceeded with his work. He did not have long, but he did not need long. He gathered the food and the ammunition—of which he had run short—together with some tobacco and matches and other items required. These articles he made into a great parcel, wrapped in a tarpaulin. Next he went into the little glade adjoining where the horses were hobbled on the grass. He selected the toughest and best weight carrier—which happened to be the mount of the ex-sheriff himself—and led the animal away, while the pack was slung over his own broad shoulder. He had reached the farther side of the pool before the man he had left behind him, stunned, recovered his senses and his wits enough to raise an outcry. Then his shout brought every member of the party to his feet.

But Bobbie was in no great hurry. He changed saddles from his worn-out mount to his new one, arranged his pack behind the saddle, cast away a few non-essentials, and then mounted and jogged along on his way. As for the men on the farther side of the pool, they had hastily mounted and then bolted for the mountains, thundering threats of vengeance—all save the poor ex-sheriff, who stayed behind, cursing the thief who had deprived him of his best horse.

They found no track of Bobbie on that day or the next. He was well away and traveling in security by a route that none discovered. In the heart of the mountains he built a large fire, cooked a great quantity of bacon and flapjacks, warmed some tinned beans, made himself a great pot of coffee, stayed awake after his feast long enough to smoke half a cigarette, and then dropped into a sound slumber that lasted a round of the clock. It was the first real sleep he had enjoyed during his flight. When he wakened again, his head was clear, his stomach was again empty, his eye was bright, and it was now that he began truly to enjoy the game in which he was engaged.

After that, the hunters who worked through the Kiever Mountains led a wretched life. By nature Bobbie was two or three long strides closer to the soil than the white men who were now his enemies. His hearing was a little sharper, his sight a little more acute, and, above all, there was more keenly developed in him that indescribable sense that does not reside in any nerves of the flesh, but in the nerves of the soul—the power, in short, of premonition. After his long sleep he was ready for mischief, and straightway he had his fun.

That afternoon three parties that had worked well into the hills glimpsed his horse, and at the same time Bobbie glimpsed them. They were coming in three different directions, and his chance of riding through was small. So he let his newly stolen horse remain behind him to keep the eyes of the enemy in focus, while he himself stole down a little gully and made off with his guns and little else besides. Half an hour later, as the baffled hunters closed on the horse and found that the master was gone, Bobbie discovered that a lone rider was jogging a fine bay stallion into the Kiever Mountains, hunting glory with his single hand. Bobbie tied that young hero's hands behind his back, did him no other harm, took his excellent mount, and made off blithely again.

He had no provisions again, however. So, on that very night, he dropped down on a party of his hunters. There were only three, and Bobbie used different methods here. He waked them up, herded them together with a few gestures of his revolvers, fastened them with two pairs of bridle reins, and then went through their belongings in the most leisurely fashion. He gained plunder enough. Hitherto he had taken only essentials. But now his eyes were caught and filled by a fine rifle, decorated with a little gold chasing. He took that weapon, while its owner groaned. Then he selected a fine hunting knife that belonged to another. Finally, though he retained the horse he was riding, he exchanged the saddle for another. He went through their stock of provisions, selected what he needed, cooked himself a meal, and then rode away through the night, singing in a rich and ringing baritone voice.

By the time the report of this affair had spread through Kiever County, the men of the district were half hysterical with rage and the desire for revenge. If forty men had been hunting the fugitive the day before, by nightfall of that day no fewer than fifty parties were laboring among the slopes of the Kiever Mountains. Still their task was not accomplished, and, indeed, it was not simple, for in every square league of the range there were enough hiding places difficult of access to employ the entire fifty hunting parties through a whole day's work. They had rushed out feeling that sheer numbers would now complete the net and make it perfect, but they saw that mere numbers would not avail them. Hard work and a little luck were what they needed.

In the meantime, to complete their anger, reporters began to ride in from various southwest cities. They wanted to have pictures of camera and pen to describe the range where the Negro was lurking. Kiever County snarled like a savage dog and quivered with rage. Then they read the stories of the reporters and grew more furious than ever. Bobbie was called a dusky-skinned Hannibal who now was showing the destructive talents of his race by setting at naught the efforts of the great odds that worked day and night against him. It was pointed out that he was a Negro with a sense of humor, and that he was not a sheer murderer, but really preferred to defend himself and leave his antagonists alive—so that he might have all the more to play with.

Such was the tone in which these articles were written. Kiever County, finding itself mentioned as giving "amusement" to a single fugitive by its combined effort to capture him, writhed in silence, and in silence it put forth fresh efforts. But still Bobbie was not taken. He was a little lean of face and a little grim of eye, but compared with his old self he was as one who has awakened from a deep sleep. He was finding himself, and what he found was all new to him.

It was now estimated that three hundred manhunters labored to find the trail of the Negro and run him down. There were packs of dogs of all descriptions. They were worked day and night. Even so, Bobbie was not caught, and even so Bobbie continued to descend upon the besiegers and prey upon them for his livelihood. All of this was noted by the merciless pens of the newspaper reporters. They talked with great and delicate sarcasm about the charity of the posses of the Kiever men, and they dilated upon the truly Christian spirit that, when men had been smitten, made them turn the other cheek to the smiter. But a new danger was drawing close to Bobbie.

VIII

When Tom Farnsworth left Deborah, his head was muddled, indeed. He had gone to see her with a high heart full of love for her. He left with his love cut off and destroyed utterly at the root. All of his hopes of happiness had been exchanged for a grisly threat that compromised his honor forever and even his very life. As he stumbled back to his horse, after he left the house, he still could not quite understand how she had tricked him into confessing the truth to her. But now he could very well understand that he had made his case far blacker than it really was by his delay. If he had come before the people of the town the very night of the shooting and told them what had happened, they might have believed him. Certainly Jack had forced the fight more than he had. Jack himself would admit it. But now Jack was following a line that he thought would be most helpful to his rival, and with a mistaken sense of honor he was continuing to let Bobbie shoulder the blame he had taken up. That was not all. Jack was now fallen into a delirium again, and he well might die before he could awaken. In that case, either Bobbie must be killed before Tom could help Bobbie, or else, failing this, the girl would accuse him and damn him.

Such was the problem Tom Farnsworth now had to work out, and after half an hour of thinking and gritting of teeth he made up his mind that there was nothing for it. He had to find Bobbie and kill him.

To do young Farnsworth justice, his head spun, and he grew sick when he thought of betraying that long-suffering servant. Yet, being by nature an opportunist, he balanced matters back and forth and argued in the following manner: *If Bobbie had not foolishly ridden away that night, I would have told the truth about the affair. As it happened, he rode away, took the blame, kept me from confessing, and now it is so late that, if I confess, I shall not be believed. Bobbie, in short, is at the root of all the mischief. And he has himself brought this matter to such a point that now I have to procure his death and make it seem as though a third person dropped him. This is all very difficult and close work, and I shall have to be more adroit than I have ever been before.*

This may seem cold-blooded reasoning, and in fact it was, but Tom was working for his life, and on such occasions even generous men with warm hearts are apt to change a little from their better natures. He went home, surprised himself by being able to sleep well, rose early the next morning, took a good horse, and started out on his journey. He went through Daggett and let his errand be known. He had gone to find his truant servant and learn what had happened to the usually sober brain of Bobbie. He had to make that announcement in Daggett in the hope that the tidings would roll before him and come to Bobbie among the Kiever Mountains, via some of the guards whom he was now harrying daily with his descents from the fastnesses of the peaks. When Bobbie learned of it, he would instantly do his best to throw himself into the path of his coming master.

Before Tom left, he heard other news. Just as he had dreaded, young Jack Pattison had grown worse almost immediately after his interview with Tom. The sweet sleep into which he had fallen had been the result, apparently, of having wrought nerves that now had snapped. The sleep changed to a nightmare. Jack Pattison wakened in a shrieking delirium, begging for Deborah, and Deborah went to him. She quieted him, but she could not bring him back to reason. She had spent the rest of the night leaning over his bed, and on this day she and the doctor and two nurses were fighting gallantly to save the youngster from death, but it seemed to be a losing fight.

It means that I must hurry, said Tom to himself. *If Bobbie and Pattison are both disposed of, the girl will tell herself that enough men have died on account of this affair. But if Pattison dies, and Bobbie is still at large, she'll speak out, and then I'm a ruined man.*

He rode furiously forward after that. On the second day he saw the Kiever Mountains, drawing out of the horizon like great blue-gray clouds. That evening he reached the mountains themselves, pressed into them until he found a camping place, and then, having unsaddled his horse, he sat down, lit a cigarette, and waited. He was as certain that Bobbie would come to him at once as he was certain that an eagle can see what a man cannot. He looked forward to that meeting with a disagreeable shudder. He decided, finally, that he would have to kill Bobbie from in front. That meant that he would have to murder his man while looking him in the eye, and even the iron nerves of Tom Farnsworth trembled at such a prospect. He must shoot Bobbie from in front. Probably he had better shoot through the head. Then it could be explained as an accident that had taken place while Bobbie himself was handling a gun.

In the midst of these black meditations he was aware of something stirring in the black of the night behind him. He turned sharply, and there was Bobbie. But how changed! He saw first a streak of red where a huge red silk bandanna was tied like a turban around the head of the Negro. Beneath that red were the gleam of eyes and the white glimmer of teeth, as Bobbie grinned delightedly down at his visitor. He wore a canvas jacket without sleeves, and his trousers had been cut off at the knees. On his feet were rudely made moccasins. About his waist was no cartridge belt—there was only the holster for the Colt, dangling from his right hip, and there was no rifle behind his shoulder. The Colt was his only weapon, and the whole outfit of the Negro seemed invented and adapted for great activity in flight rather than power to stand and give battle. But the appearance of Bobbie was not the only wild thing about him. He danced like a wild man when he saw his master and broke into frantic protestations of delight. That very morning he had come down in the gray of the dawn upon a camp, taken a supply of coffee that he needed, and carried away with him a young cowpuncher from whom he had extracted all manner of information about the number of his assailants, the plans of the sheriff, and, above all, the tidings that his master, Tom Farnsworth, was on the way to take a hand in this matter and bring the fugitive to justice.

As he reached this point in his narrative, Bobbie rocked back and forth in his place in an ecstasy of silent mirth. He made Tom Farnsworth think of a big, sleek-muscled panther.

"Where's your horse?" he asked the big Negro.

"In the hollow," said the other.

"Your rifle?"

"I don't use one."

"Nor a coat?"

"I travel light. I can't fight three hundred men, but I can run away from them. A rifle is heavy. I carry six shots in a revolver and a few more in a pocket. That's enough. I only fire one a day at game and another one for practice. And so far I haven't had to use guns on men very often."

"Bobbie, you seem happy."

"As a king, sir."

"You haven't lost much weight or sleep, I see."

"Not a particle."

He has gone back to Nature, Farnsworth thought to himself. *The rascal has reverted to his old and true type. He has turned from a perfect servant into a perfect devil. And why,* he added to himself, *should I keep my scruples when I'm dealing with this wild man?* He said aloud: "Let me have that gun."

He could hardly believe his eyes when he saw that Bobbie hesitated nervously before he surrendered the required weapon, as though a slight suspicion of what his master intended may have flashed across his mind. But he shook his head, shrugged the fear away, and passed over the Colt.

Now, Farnsworth thought, *I have him in my hand . . . I have only to press this trigger . . .* He looked up squarely and suddenly into the man's face. "Bobbie," he said, "do you know what's in my mind?"

The mirth and the recklessness had faded out of the face of Bobbie. He stood very stiffly erect with his arms folded high on his breast. "I've a sort of an idea, sir," said Bobbie dryly.

"Your idea is right, let me tell you."

"I hope not, sir."

"Have you ever worked for me simply because you thought I was a good man, Bobbie?"

"Good, sir?" echoed Bobbie, rolling his eyes as the thought struck him for the first time.

"No," concluded the master, "of course, you haven't. You've always known in your heart of hearts that I was a rascal. Yes, you've always known that, Bobbie, and the reason you've kept true to me and my needs is simply that you'd had the old example stuffed down your throat by your granddaddy. Am I right?"

"Maybe you are, sir."

He saw the hand of Bobbie slide down. The thumb hooked into his belt. The fingers disappeared into the side pocket, and into the mind of Tom flashed understanding. The Negro had curled his fingers around the handle of the hunting knife, and, if he fought for his life, it would be by throwing that heavy and deadly weapon at Tom.

"I know," said Tom, "a knife is good for close work like this, but it's hardly fast enough. A bullet beats it from the start so far that it really hasn't a man-size chance. You understand me? Here I am with your gun in one hand and my own"—drawing it—"in the other. I think that I have you fairly at my mercy, Bobbie. Let me tell you, in the first place, why it's necessary for me to do this. It isn't a matter of careless wish. I'd rather lose a leg than lose you, Bobbie. But matters have come to such a point that I have to lose you or myself. I'm very fond of you . . . far fonder than you really dream. But, much as I like you, I confess that I prefer my own life. Matters have come to such a point, Bobbie, that I have to choose between us, and my choice is myself. If you die, all is well. If I die, there will be one less rascal in the world. As for the shabby treatment I'm giving you . . . well, I'll answer for that in hell, where I suppose I'm tolerably certain to pull up. So, to make an end of the talking . . . Bobbie, good-bye. If you've got a prayer to say, say it, because this is the end of your time."

The Negro merely stiffened in his place. "Shoot straight, Mister Tom," he said quietly. "Don't let that gun pull to the right, the way you mostly always do."

"Curse you!" gasped Tom Farnsworth.

The bright, black eyes glittered back at him as steadily as the light along the shining barrel of his Colt. So, with an oath, the white man threw the revolver down on the ground at Bobbie's feet.

"I can't do it," said Tom.

"Thank God!" cried the big Negro. "I knew you couldn't, sir. I . . ." He made as though to throw himself at the feet of Tom in an excess of his joy, but the white man repulsed him with a sharp word.

"I'm not through. I've simply changed my mind about you, Bobbie. I find that I haven't as steady a nerve as I thought I had. I can't murder you in cold blood. But I'll fight you with an equal chance between us."

The Negro frowned. "Mister Tom, you've seen me use a gun."

"I've seen you chip twigs off trees and knock the heads off ground squirrels at thirty yards . . . I've seen you do all the tricks, Bobbie, but there is no trick in this. And I'll put myself against yourself in this manner of fight. There's your gun at your feet. Pick it up!"

Bobbie stooped, grasped the revolver, and stood straight again.

"Are you ready, Bobbie?"

"Yes, sir."

"Don't call me sir. Damn me . . . curse me. I'm trying to steal your life, Bobbie. I'm trying to take that on top of twenty years of slavish service for me. I'm trying to take your life after I've beaten you before strangers . . . like a dog. Remember these things. Now, Bobbie, are you ready?"

"Ready, sir."

The white man scowled, then he shrugged his shoulders. "Shoot to kill, Bobbie," he warned the other. "If you only wing me, I'll keep blazing away until the last spark is out in me. Now, Bobbie, stoop with me and put your gun down at your feet once more. So! Now we stand once more and consider what we have to do. I begin to count ten. When I hit the last count, we dive for our Colts and open fire. You understand? Is that fair to you as it is to me?"

"Yes, sir," said Bobbie.

"For pity's sake, man," broke out Tom, "is there no malice in you? Have you nothing to say about this life of yours, which I'm trying to waste after you freely put it in such danger for me, Bobbie?"

"I've nothing to say, sir."

The master swore to himself, first very softly, then very loudly, as though he needed all that violence to waken his own courage and bring it hotly up to the point of swift action. Then he began to count. He tolled out the numbers, as regularly as a bell strikes. He reached nine and trembled with eagerness. He reached ten, snatched up his Colt with one frantically swift gesture, and fired without lifting his hand from the ground. His finger was already closing on the trigger when he saw that Bobbie had not stirred in his place. His arms were still folded stiffly and high across his chest, and he had not stooped an inch toward the gun at his feet. Too late Tom strove to check that curling of his finger. But his whole hand had gripped at gun butt and trigger, and he groaned as the revolver exploded.

"I've missed!" cried Tom, hurling his gun far away from him. "Thank heaven, I missed you, Bobbie!"

For Bobbie had not stirred in his place. "A mighty neat shot, sir," said Bobbie. "But the head is the thing to aim at, even with a snap shot. The body will do only once in a while." He pushed open his canvas jacket and thrust his hand into his bosom. He brought it out again with the fingers stained crimson. "This time," said Bobbie, "I think that it will do very nicely."

Then he crumpled, as though the force of the bullet had torn into him at that moment. The arms of Tom caught at him, but that huge bulk of solid bone and muscle glided through his hands like an avalanche and came to rest heavily against the earth. The canvas jacket was ripped away. The jet-black chest was exposed, arched like a noble dome, and splashed with the thick red.

The white man beat his hands together and then dashed them against his face. He tore off his shirt and started to tear it into strips for bandages. Then he stopped to take the big head of the Negro in his arms and groan: "Bobbie, Bobbie, I've killed you! It was the devil, Bobbie, not I."

"Steady," whispered a faint voice from the ground. "Tell them that you were cleaning your own gun . . . they won't care, except that I belonged to you, and they'll wonder why you threw me away."

IX

"No talk," breathed Tom Farnsworth. "Save your strength . . . save your strength, Bobbie."

"Yes, sir," murmured the Negro.

Farnsworth was working like mad, twisting the bandages into place, stripping his body for that purpose, shivering not with the cold of the mountain night but with the icy fears that were whispering at his shoulder. For, as he worked, he was looking deep, deep into the truth about himself and the truth about the man he'd shot. *What if Bobbie died?* At that thought a thousand pictures leaped across his mind. There was time for many memories in every fraction of a second. And every recollection was of Bobbie in some other day, and in each one of those other days Bobbie was serving him more faithfully than any brother, more humbly than any slave.

He finished the bandaging. He rushed down the slope to the brink of the little spring and brought back a canteen of water. When he returned, the eyes of the Negro were closed, and the heart of Tom Farnsworth sank in him. But he recalled that men in death open their eyes for the last time. It was only a fainting fit. So he poured some water down the throat of Bobbie and had the sad gratification of hearing Bobbie groan and seeing his eyelids flicker.

Then he was up on his feet again and working frantically. There was a growth of young pine saplings near the spring. He fell upon them with his hatchet, which he carried behind his saddle, and felled them one and all. With some he built a roaring fire, partly to keep away the cold and partly because he felt that he needed light and warmth to fight away death, which had stolen close to his servant in the darkness. With the tips and the needles of the saplings he constructed a deep and soft bed, over which he spread his tarpaulin and then fell to the labor of moving the big, wounded man to this new position of comfort. There followed five minutes of agony of effort, for Tom was not strong, and the inert bulk of Bobbie almost baffled all of his pulling and straining. There could be no roughness. All must be done smoothly, easily. When it was accomplished, he looked anxiously at the bandage, fearful lest it might have shown a new spurting of blood. But the bandage showed only the one dark spot.

He now covered Bobbie with a saddle blanket and moistened his lips with a dram of brandy from his pocket flask. Bobbie opened his eyes again, sighed, and looked with a faint smile upon his master. The white man took advantage of this glimmer of returning consciousness to make a desperate appeal.

"You're not nearly gone, partner," he said. "Keep on fighting, Bobbie. Don't let it get you. Here we are, shoulder to shoulder, fighting the same fight. Can it beat the two of us when we are making a hard fight, old man? Good old Bobbie. Don't answer me with a word. Just lift the forefinger of your hand to let me know."

"Yes, sir," whispered Bobbie, and his smile broadened to an ecstasy of happiness. Then his smile died, and his eyes closed once more, while his face wrinkled in a spasm of pain.

"He's dead!" gasped Tom Farnsworth. He looked wildly about him, but what was there he could do? He had felt, up to this point, that he had been fighting valiantly and successfully against death. He had felt that he was almost as strong as death itself in this great battle. But now there was no longer anything with which he could employ his hands. He could only sit and look about him at the greatness and the blackness of the night and up the brawny sides of the mountain, so utterly indifferent to this trifling human misery. There was nothing he could do except to throw more wood upon the fire. That light might prove a beacon that would bring in the hunters upon them both. But he desired nothing more. Let them come, and he might find among them a doctor who could be of direct help in this emergency.

He started up and threw more fuel on the blaze. The pitchy needles cast towering masses of red fire high into the air. The wood itself caught and flared grandly. Then, troubled with a new thought, he turned and knelt beside Bobbie to shield his eyes from the play and shaking of the columns of light. Once the Negro opened his eyes and looked up calmly with no dimness of faded strength.

"Bobbie," whispered the master, "will you forgive me, my friend?"

Before even an assent of expression could cross the face of Bobbie, the life had died in his eyes once more, and he passed into an utter faint. Farnsworth was furiously at work over him in a trice. There was another taste of brandy and water, then chafing of the Negro's temples—not that he really expected that this would help, but because he must either do something, or else go mad with the suspense.

As he worked, he felt barriers broken down, one by one, in his heart. He began to remember a thousand instances of cruelty on his part and of bitter neglect of Bobbie. He began to recall the gentle dignity of Bobbie in all the years of service that the Negro had poured out like a slave in service to the Farnsworth family. And then shame, grief, the deepest remorse for what he had done, and what he had been, swept over him. He looked upon the thing that he had been yesterday with a sort of horror, as though these had been the doings of strangers, and unworthy strangers at that. That he could have allowed this worthy fellow to ride away, carrying the burden and the danger of a charge of murder on his shoulders, was now incomprehensible, though then he had no more than shrugged his shoulders and called Bobbie a fool to himself.

When the doors of self-knowledge are once opened, we are too apt to see far deeper into our souls than we had intended or ever guessed. He saw a great deal about himself in the first glance, and nearly everything was damning. His college career, of whose dissipations he had been rather proud, he now looked back upon as a wasted season of foolishness in which he had prided himself merely because of the difference that had existed between himself and other people. Such were some of the reflections of Tom Farnsworth. But worse than this and coming nearer to the present, he could now see that the reason Deborah Kinkaid had been so attractive to him was simply because she had refused to be awed by his presence. She had kept him at arm's length, and for that reason she had at once seemed to him far pleasanter than any girl he had seen. He thought of this grimly, then with something of a shudder. Suppose that he had married her and awakened later on? Yet it was presumptuous to suppose that she would even have considered accepting him as a husband. But to learn all these things he had had to bring poor Bobbie to the gate of death. The second man within a few days. He sat up straight as the thought drove home in him. *Was the very instinct of murder in him, then?*

That thought faded into a reality of forms that stood before him. One—two—three—sneaking up toward him, with guns in their hands. He turned his head another way. There were twenty men circling in upon him. He raised his hand.

"Any one of you fellows a doctor?" he asked.

Then they came hurrying in. They looked at him. They looked at Bobbie. Then they cursed softly, eyeing him as though he were a leper.

"You did this, Farnsworth?" asked one gray-headed man with a young face. "I thought that Bobbie was your servant?"

"Friends," said Farnsworth, "I came here to meet Bobbie, and, while we were looking over a gun, it exploded."

He saw faint smiles of contempt and derision in their faces. In the old days—that is to say, an hour before that—he would have scoffed at such expressions from the boors of the cattle range. But now every man was a man, no matter what his breeding or his manners. And their opinions stung him like so many whips. A doctor was brought forward. He was a veterinary in practice, but much more a rancher. He had some knowledge of anatomy, and his hands had taken care of scores of wounded men in his day. Therefore, he was soon beside the unconscious figure of Bobbie. While he worked to give an opinion of the nature of the hurt, the others stood around and rolled their cigarettes. They made few comments, but those were to the point. One man, noting the long, rounded, smooth-muscled arm of the Negro, swore that he could now understand why Bobbie had handled grown cowpunchers as though they were children. Another, staring at the unconscious face of the wounded man, said that there was only one black thing about him, and that was his skin.

"What's more," said the cowpuncher with the gray hair, "we'd never have taken him except for . . ." He turned with a gesture to Tom and an ugly look to complete his thought.

The doctor now rose to his feet, dusting his hands together and frowning down at the victim. His eyes were keen. "He's dead."

There was a mutter and a sharp exclamation of pain from Tom Farnsworth, so real, so ringing, that the cowpunchers, who had made up their minds about him, it seemed, now stared at him with a new interest.

"Dead?" cried Tom.

"I say he's dead!" barked the doctor. "Anyways, he ought to be dead. That chunk of lead carved right straight through him. Why he ain't foaming blood at the mouth I dunno . . . why he ain't dead right now, I dunno. But here he is, living and calling me the same's a liar. And if he ain't dead or dying right this minute, maybe there's a hope for him. He's got to be treated plumb careful."

"He'll have all the care in the world!" exclaimed Tom.

The sheriff yawned. "We got to get him to jail," he said.

"For horse stealing?" asked Tom.

"That's part."

"I'll pay every man's claim."

"Will you pay the claim of poor young Pattison, dying over to Daggett?"

"There's no blame on Bobbie for that."

"Are you aiming to tell me my business, young man?" said the sheriff, who like most of the men on the range had heard of the eccentricities of young Farnsworth and greatly disliked all that he knew of the latter.

"I'll tell you what Bobbie did," said Tom. "He took the blame of another man on his shoulders."

"That sounds likely. Run his head into a noose for the sake of somebody else, eh?"

"I mean it, Sheriff."

"Look here, Mister Farnsworth"—and those the sheriff called by that formal title could be sure they rested under his disapproval—"your pa is a smart man. I've knowed him well and thought a lot of him. But even your pa couldn't have me swallow such bunk as that. You been to college, Mister Farnsworth, which is an advantage that I ain't never had, but I thank my Maker that I can use the few brains He give me better than to believe any yarn like that."

"Sheriff," said Tom, "I can name the man who shot Jack Pattison."

"So can everybody west of the Mississippi. It's Bobbie."

"It is not."

"Let's have your guess then, son."

The others waited, and the sheriff smiled wisely upon them, and they smiled wisely back upon the sheriff, for it would be pleasant to have this youth with his superior airs brought to time.

"I did," said Tom.

The smiles wavered and then went out, like candles snuffed by a rudely unexpected wind.

"Are you making a joke out of me, Farnsworth?"

"It's the truth, Sheriff. I shot Jack. He's kept the secret for my sake."

"Look here," muttered the sheriff, "you mean to say that you shot Pattison, and then let your man here ride off with the blame for the killing?"

It was exquisite agony for Tom, but he swallowed the medicine and felt it burn home in him. "I did," he answered.

"I'm a tolerable reasonable man," said the sheriff, "but I got to admit free and quick that this here plumb beats me. Which I aim to hear you talk some more about, Farnsworth. You let him go, but then you come after him?"

"I did."

"Wanted to change places with him, maybe?"

"No."

"Why didn't you let well enough alone?"

"I wanted to get more out of him," said Tom bitterly, and all at once, as he found in himself the strength to confess, he found the strength, also, to lift his head and look around on those grave, weather-chiseled faces.

"More than what he'd done?"

"Yes."

"What was it, Tom?" asked the sheriff. His gentleness was amazing.

He's trying to draw me out, thought Tom. He said aloud: "There was still one more thing that Bobbie could do for me."

"And that?"

"Die, as Pattison was doing, and take my secret away with him."

The sheriff gasped. "You admit then . . . ?"

"Everything," said Tom.

"You're under arrest, Tom!" cried the sheriff. "For the Lord's sake, man, mind that everything you say now can be used against you."

"I mind it very well."

"You confess that you shot Jack Pattison?"

"I do."

"That you let Bobbie take the blame of it?"

"I do."

"That you come out here to get rid of the man that had risked his head for you?"

"I confess it," groaned Tom.

"And that, when you met him, you shot him down?"

"God have mercy on me," replied Tom solemnly, "as I expect nothing but justice on earth . . . I confess this, too."

The silence of the men weighed upon him like lead. He turned desperate eyes upon the wide circle of their faces, and he saw with amazement that they were looking upon him rather with surprise than with horror or anger.

"Tom," said the sheriff slowly at last, "dog-gone me if I quite make you out. Being and talking like a white man this hour, how could you have played the skunk one hour back?"

And that, on the whole, was the general opinion of the entire cattle range. It was freely expressed that day and the next, while Tom Farnsworth was being brought to Daggett to sleep in the jail.

X

The news came like a bomb to Daggett. It affected people with one emotion—astonishment. They could not believe that the son of Thomas Farnsworth was guilty of a shooting scrape. When they heard it confirmed, they could not understand how Tom Farnsworth had been induced to confess to his double crime. They heard of other things, also. On the way into town he was

not moved to mention his own welfare once, but he was thinking and talking every moment of ways in which the comfort of
Bobbie could be increased while he lay on the mountainside. In
the first place, he had furnished an ample supply of cash to buy
all sorts of provisions. They had secured enough tarpaulins from
the cowpunchers to erect a little tent for the wounded Negro.
Then the veterinary and two cowpunchers were hired to act as
nurses until more aid could be sent out from the town, together
with bandages and all manner of medical necessities, for it was
beyond question that it would kill Bobbie to move him. So young
Farnsworth planned to build a house over him, so to speak, and
turn that spot on the mountainside into a little hospital.

As for his own trial, he refused to speak except to say that
he had confessed everything and would confess it again. He felt
that he had downed Pattison in a fair fight, and, as for Bobbie,
nothing could save Tom if the Negro perished. He wished to
have the law executed to the letter upon his person.

These were the strange sentiments that were expressed by
Tom on his way back to Daggett. His father met him at the
jail, throwing himself off a foaming horse and rushing into the
building in spite of the sheriff.

"You have disgraced your family and me forever!" he had
cried to his son.

"Farnsworth," said the sheriff, "you're wrong. He's just proved
that he's a credit to you all. By the Lord, Farnsworth, I wish he
were my boy."

This was much quoted around the streets the next day. Still
more repeated was the interview between Bobbie's grandfather
and young Tom the next morning. The ancient Negro had hobbled into the jail, supporting himself on a cane with one hand
and fumbling his way along the wall with the other. He had been
straight as a string the day before. He was bent as a bow now.
He had grown decrepit overnight. When he saw his master's boy
behind the bars, he fell on his knees and burst into pitiful sobbing.

"Marse Tom! Marse Tom," groaned the old fellow. "Lawdy, Lawdy! I knowed that Bobbie would be a trouble and a harm to you."

"Hush, uncle," said the prisoner, coming to the bars of his cell. "Bobbie has done more for me than all the rest of the world together could ever have done. He's taught me what men are."

"He's brought you to ruin, Marse Tom."

"Let me tell you what he has done, uncle," said the other. "He's taught me that a man who thinks that he's worthy of being a master is not fit to be even a slave. He taught me that he is a far better man than I am."

Tidings of this odd conversation were brought to Deborah Kinkaid, where she labored night and day at the bedside of Jack Pattison. She had made up her mind, at last. Jack was to be her husband, if she could win him back to life. She had told him so, and he was fighting with his whole strength to aid in the battle. The doctor said that it was being won from a reluctant enemy, step by step. She heard that report and turned straightway to the window and looked out at the morning sunlight, glistening on the roofs of Daggett.

"I half guessed it before," she murmured, "but only half. I didn't know he had such a thing in him."

And she sighed, but, if it were with a regret, Jack Pattison was never to know. He began to recover rapidly. By that night he was out of danger.

Still another week passed before word came from the Kiever Mountains that the big Negro was also recovering slowly. All of Daggett came down to give Tom Farnsworth a cheer in the jail. He listened to the noise with amazement, and the sheriff came in to explain.

"When a man shows that he's white," said the sheriff, "all the black things that he's ever done before are washed away and forgotten. That's the way with you, Tom. I'm going to bust the law ten ways from Sunday. You're free this minute. Go outside. Your father is waiting to take you home."

Outside, Tom walked into an ovation. He received it with his head bared and bowed, and he rode all the way out to the ranch at his father's side without answering a word to that fine old gentleman's exultation.

"Now," said Thomas Farnsworth, Sr., "when you have all the fool nonsense worked out of your head, you can settle right down on the ranch and get ready to take charge when I'm ready to step out, which will be plenty *pronto*."

It was not until the next morning that Tom, Jr. came to make his reply at the breakfast table. He was dressed not for the ranch, but for travel, and he explained this condition at once.

"Father," he said to the old man, "I've decided that I don't want the ranch, and that the ranch doesn't want me."

"What the devil sort of talk is this?" roared the rancher.

"Straight talk."

"What do you intend to do, then?"

"Start with these clothes on my back and fifty dollars in my pocket and see where it takes me. Then buck my own way with my own hands."

"You learned that out of some fool book."

The son smiled and said no more.

"You mean," shouted his father, "that you're not coming back?"

"I don't mean that. I'll come back when I can tell you something that I've done besides spend your money."

"The ranch is to go to pot, eh?"

"You don't need help, and you know it. If you do, I can give you a proved man to take my place and do better than I could ever have done."

"Who's that?"

"Bobbie."

With that the talk was brought to a sudden close. That very day young Tom rode away from his home. He avoided Daggett, simply because he did not want to be run after and congratulated. He felt a warm shame and a weakness in his throat when he thought of the average goodness of human beings who could overlook and forget the harm he had done. He set the head of his horse toward the Kiever Mountains, far north and west, for one last talk with Bobbie. And he wondered, as he went on, what he would find in the big Negro, when he looked on him as a free man and not as a slave, and what would Bobbie find in him, now that he was no longer the master?

A Lucky Dog

"A Lucky Dog" first appeared in the October 22, 1927 issue of Street & Smith's *Western Story Magazine*. That year also saw the publication of eleven other short novels and eight serials, all but three appearing in *Western Story Magazine*. It is an unusual and charming story infused with Faust's love for white bull terriers.

I

When at last Hagger was inside the shop, he paused and listened to the rush of the rain against the windows. Then he turned to the jeweler with a faint smile of possession, for the hardest part of the job was over before he had opened the door to enter the place. During the days that went before he had studied the entrances and exits, the value of the contents of the place, and, when he cut the wires that ran to the alarm, he knew that the work was finished.

So he advanced, and to conceal any touch of grimness in his approach he made his smile broader and said: "Evening, Mister Friedman."

The young man nodded with mingled anxiety and eagerness, as though he feared loss and hoped for gain even before a bargain was broached.

"How much for this?" Hagger said, and slipped a watch onto the counter.

The other drew back, partly to bring the watch under a brighter light, and partly to put a little distance between himself and this customer, for Hagger was too perfectly adapted to his part. One does not need to be told that the bull terrier is a fighting dog, and the pale face of Hagger, square about the jaws and lighted by a cold and steady eye, was too eloquent.

All of this Hagger knew, and he made a little pleasant conversation. "You're young to be holding down a swell joint like this," he observed.

The young man snapped open the back of the watch and observed the mechanism—one eye for it and one for his customer. "About two dollars," he said. "I got this place from my father," he added in explanation.

"Two dollars? Have a heart!" Hagger grinned. "I'll tell you what I paid. I paid twenty-two dollars for it."

"There are lots of rascals in the business," said Friedman, and he made a wry face at the thought of them.

"I got it," said Hagger, raising his voice in increasing anger, "right down the street at Overman's. Twenty-two bucks. I'll let it go for twelve, though. That's a bargain for you, Friedman."

Mr. Friedman closed the watch, breathed upon it, and rubbed off an imaginary fleck of dust with the cuff of his linen shop coat, already blackened by similar touches. Then he pushed the watch softly across the counter with both hands and shook his head, smiling.

"You think I want to rob you. No, I want people to keep coming back here. Two dollars, maybe two-fifty. That's the limit."

"You're kidding," observed Hagger, his brow darker than before.

"I got to know my business," declared Friedman. "I've been at it since I was ten, working and studying. I know watches." He added, pointing: "Look at that case. Look at that yellow spot. That's the brass wearing through. It'd be hard to sell that watch across the counter, mister."

"Well, gimme the coin. All you birds . . . you all work together to soak the rest of us. It's easy money for you."

Friedman shrugged his eloquent shoulders and turned to the cash register. "Here you are," he said as he swung back, money in hand.

Hagger struck at that moment. Some people use the barrel of a revolver for such work; some use the brutal butt, or a slung shot of massive lead. But Hagger knew that a little sandbag of just the right weight was fully as effective and never smashed bones—fully as effective, that is, if one knew just where to tap with it. Hagger knew as well as any surgeon.

The young man fell back against the wall. His little handful of silver clattered on the floor as he went limp. For a moment he regarded Hagger with stupid eyes, and then began to sink. Hagger vaulted lightly across the counter, lowered his man, and stretched him out comfortably. He even delayed to draw up an eyelid and consider the light in the eye beneath. Then, satisfied that he had produced no more than a moment of sleep, he went to work.

He knew beforehand that there was very little value in the material displayed, compared with its bulk and weight. All that was of worth was contained in the two trays of the central case—watches and rings, and in particular a pair of bracelets of square-faced emeralds. A little pale and a little flawed were those stones, but still they were worth something.

He dumped the contents of the two trays into his coat pockets, and then he walked out the back way. The door was locked, and there was no key in it, but he was not disturbed. He braced his shoulder against it and thrust the weight home. There was only a slight scraping sound, and the door sagged open and let the rain drive in.

He was so little in a hurry that he paused to look up to the lights and the roar of an elevated train crashing past. Then he walked lightly down the street, turned over to Lexington at the next block, and caught a southbound taxi. At Third Street he stopped, and then walked back two blocks and turned in at a narrow entrance.

The tinkle of the shop bell brought a looming figure clad in black, greasy with age.

"Hullo, Steffans."

"Hullo, Hagger. Buy or sell tonight, kid?"

"I sell, bo."

The big man laughed silently and ushered the customer into a back room. "Lemme see," he urged, and put his hands on the edge of a table covered with green felt.

"Nothing much," said Hagger, "but safety first, y'understand? Big dough for big chances. I'm going light lately."

After this apology, he dumped his loot on the table, and Steffans touched it with expert fingers.

"Chicken feed, chicken feed," he said. "But I'm glad to have it. I could handle a truck load of this sort of stuff every day and the damned elbows would never bother me."

"Go on," said Hagger.

"You want to make a move," said Steffans. "You're always in a hurry after a job. Look at some of the other boys, though. They never attempt to leave town."

"Except for the can," said Hagger.

Steffans settled himself before the little heap and pulled his magnifying glass down from his forehead. "That's right," he said. "You never been up the river. You got the luck."

"I got the brains," corrected Hagger. "Some saps work with their hands. Brains are what count. Brains, and crust like yours, Steffans, you robber."

"I get a high percentage," said Steffans, "but then I always mark 'em up a full value. Y'understand? I'll give you seventy on this batch, Hagger."

"Seventy for me after what I've done," sighed Hagger, "and you sit here and swallow thirty for nothing."

Steffans smiled. "I've done a couple of stretches myself," he said. "You know the dicks make life hell for me. Now, I'll give you seventy percent on this stuff. Wait till I finish valuing it."

He began to go through the items swiftly, looking aside now and then to make swift calculation, while Hagger watched in admiration. Of all the fences, Steffans was the king, for the percentage he took was high, but the prices he gave were a little better than full. So he sat in his dark little pawnshop and drew toward himself vast loot collected by second-story men, pickpockets, yeggs of all descriptions.

"This isn't so bad, kid," he said, "and I'll put the whole thing down at eleven thousand. That'll give you seven thousand and seven hundred. Take you as far as Pittsburgh, I guess?"

"It's more than I expected," said Hagger instantly. "But what do I have to take instead of cash?"

"Not a damn' thing. I got a payment in just a few minutes ago. Hold on a minute."

He disappeared and came back with a bundle of paper money in his hand. Of this he counted out the specified amount and then swept all the stolen jewels into a small canvas bag.

"Is that all, Hagger?"

"That's all."

"So long, then. What was the dump?"

"No place you know, hardly likely. So long, Steffans. Here's where I blow."

He said good-bye to the pawnbroker, and, stepping out onto the sidewalk, he crashed full against the hurrying form of one about to enter—a tall, young man, and, by the light from within, Hagger made out the features of Friedman.

It startled him. Nothing but a sort of magic intuition could have brought the jeweler to such a place in his hunt for the robber. Or had Steffans relaxed his precautions lately and allowed the rank and file to learn about his secret business?

This he thought of on the instant, and at the same time there was the glitter of a gun shoved into his face, and a hoarse voice of rage and joy sounding at his ear.

"The hand is faster than the gun," Hagger was fond of saying.

He struck Friedman to the wet pavement and doubled swiftly around the corner.

II

Something that Steffans had said now brought a destination to Hagger's mind, and he took a taxi to Penn Station and bought a ticket for Pittsburgh. There was a train out in thirty minutes, and Hagger waited securely in the crowd until the gatekeeper came walking up behind the bars. Gatekeeper?

"Oh, damn his fat face!" snarled Hagger. "It's Buckholz of the Central Office. May he rot in hell!" Past Buckholz he dared not go, and, therefore, he left Penn Station, regretting the useless ticket, for he was a thrifty soul, was Hagger.

There are more ways out of New York than out of a sieve. Hagger got the night boat for Albany, and slept heavily almost until the time to dock. Then he dressed in haste and went down on deck as the mass formed at the head of the gangplank.

It amused Hagger and waked him up to sidle through that mob, and he managed it so dexterously that it was always some other person, rather than he, who received the black looks of those he jostled. He sifted through until he was among the first near the head of the broad gangplank, and the next moment he wished that he were in any other place, for on the edge of the wharf he saw the long, yellow face of Friedman, and his bright black eyes seemed to be peering up at him.

There was no use trying to turn back. At that moment the barrier was removed, and the crowd poured down, carrying Hagger swiftly on its broad current. They joined the mass that waited on the platform.

Suddenly a voice screamed: "Officer! Look! It's him!"

It was Friedman, that damned Friedman, again.

"If I ever get out of this," muttered Hagger, who habitually spoke his more important thoughts aloud, "I'll kill you." He began to work frantically through the crowd to the side, and he saw the uplifted nightstick of a policeman, trying to drive in toward him.

Out of the mass, he began to run. He knew all about running through a scattered mob, just as he knew how to work like quicksilver through a denser one. Now he moved at such a rate that the most talented of open-field runners would have gaped in amazement to see this prodigious dodging.

He found a line of taxicabs, leaped over the hood of one, darted up the line, vaulted back over the bonnet of a second, paced at full speed down a lane, and presently sat swinging his legs from the tailboard of a massive truck that rumbled toward the center of town.

"That's all right for a breather," said Hagger, "and a guy needs an appetite, when he's packing about eight grand."

He pitched on a small restaurant and, with several newspapers, sat down to his meal. He had not touched food since the previous morning, and Hagger could eat not only for the past but for the future. He did now.

The waiter, bright with admiration, hung over the table. "What wouldn't I give for an appetite like that," he said. "I suppose that you ain't had that long?"

Hagger, looking up curiously, observed that the waiter was pointing with a soiled forefinger, and at the same time winking broadly.

What could be wrong? With the most childish asininity, Hagger had allowed his coat to fall open, and from the inside pocket the wallet was revealed, and the closely packed sheaf of bills!

He was far too wary to button it at once, and went on with his breakfast. Yet, from the corner of his omniscient eye, he was keenly aware of the tall waiter talking with the proprietor, whose gestures seemed to say: "What business is it of ours?"

What a shame that there are not more men like that in the world, to make life worth living.

He sank deeper into his papers over another cup of coffee. He preferred the metropolitan journals, for by delving into them he picked up—sometimes in scattered paragraphs, sometimes in mere allusions, but sometimes in the rich mines and masses of police news spread over many sheets—the information of the world in which he moved. So he observed, for instance, that Slim Chaffer, the second-story man, had broken jail in Topeka; and that Pie Winters was locked up for forgery in Denver; and that Babe McGee had been released because of lack of evidence. At this he fairly shook with delicious mirth. For what a guy the Babe was—slippery, grinning, good-natured, and crooked past belief. Lack of evidence? Why, you never could get evidence on the Babe. Not even when he was stacking the cards on you.

To think of such a man was an inspiration to Hagger. He finished his coffee. Then he paid the bill and put down exactly ten percent for the waiter. "For you, kid," he said significantly.

Then Hagger stepped onto the pavement and walked slowly down the street, turning his thoughts slowly, meditation slackened by the vastness of his meal.

What loomed largest in his mind was: *The man was instantly identified by Friedman, from photographs, who asserted that it could be no other than Hagger, better known as "Hagger, the Yegg," whose operations in cracking safes and raiding jewelry stores are always carried out with consummate neatness and precision. The simplicity of his work is the sign of this master criminal. The police are now hard on his trail, which is expected to lead out of town.*

Every word of that article pleased Hagger. Especially he retasted and relished much: *consummate neatness, precision, master criminal*. A wave of warmth spread through Hagger's soul, and he felt a tender fondness for the police who would describe him in such a fashion. They were pretty good fellows, along their own lines. They were all right, damn them.

He strolled on in imagination, wandering into the heaven of his highest ambition, which was to stand before the world as a great international crook, whose goings and comings would be watched for by the police of half a dozen nations. Already he had done something to expand his horizon, and a trip to England and then as far as Holland had filled his mind with the jargons of foreign tongues, but it also had filled his pockets with the weight of foreign money. So, returning one day to Europe, he would visit Italy and France, and perhaps learn a little frog talk, and come back and knock out the eyes of the boys by slinging a little *parlez-vous*.

After all, it was going to be pretty hot, the life that Hagger led. When he thought of the fortunes that must eventually sift through his powerful hands, he raised his head a little and such a light came into his eyes that even the passers-by along the street glanced sharply at him and gave him room. For he looked half inspired and half devilish.

Something clanged down the street—a police patrol wagon—brakes screamed—men leaped to the ground. By heaven, they actually were hunting Hagger with police patrols; it seemed that he no longer was worth the pursuit of brilliant plainclothes men. Hagger lingered a second to digest this idea and to take note of the long, eager face of Friedman.

"I'll kill that Yid," declared Hagger, and bolted down an alleyway.

Shots boomed down the lane, and the zing of the bullets, as they passed, made Hagger leap like a hunted rabbit. But as he darted down onto the next main street, a taxi passed, and, although it was traveling at nearly full speed, Hagger hooked onto it. For he knew every trick of traffic. At the end of two blocks, the driver pulled up and began to curse him, but Hagger departed with a laugh.

A whole block behind him were the police, and a block in a crowded city was almost as good as a mile to Hagger. He gained the railroad yards, and there slipped past three or four detectives who, he could have sworn, had been posted there to stop him. Again the heart of Hagger warmed with a singular gratitude, for the police of Albany certainly were doing him proud.

If I'd been a murderer . . . a poisoner or something, or a grand counterfeiter, maybe . . . they couldn't have done any more for me, Hagger thought as he stretched himself on the rods of an express. *Nope. Not even if I'd killed the President, say, they couldn't have done any more for me.*

He laughed cheerfully as the train shuddered, and then began to roll. He would have to face freezing cold at high speed, clad only in a thin suit; he would have to endure flying cinders, cutting gravel, and all the misery of that way of travel. But he knew all about this beforehand, and he knew that he could meet the pain and endure it.

So he began that journey that eventually shunted him into Denver, and he descended in ragged, greasy clothes and with a light heart to enjoy the beauties of the mountain city. But as he came out of the station yard he was aware of a vaguely familiar figure leaning against a lamppost apparently lost in thought.

It was Friedman.

III

That figure struck Hagger's imagination as a fist strikes across a lowered guard, for it could not be the Jew, and yet there he stood, wholly absorbed in thought, and his coat was drawn so tightly around him that Hagger distinctly saw the outline of a revolver in a hip pocket.

That removed all sense of the unearthly, and Hagger slipped away toward the center of the town, more worried than he had ever been before. At a lunch counter, he meditated on this strange adventure.

Hagger knew something about Friedman, for, when he prepared for a job, he was as thorough as could be, and his questions had brought him much information about the proprietor of the shop. There was nothing in the least unusual about his rise, for his father had owned the place before him and had educated him in the rear workroom and behind the counter. High school, a little touch of bookishness, perhaps, which generally simply unnerves a man. What was there in this background to prepare Friedman for his feat of trailing an elusive criminal more than halfway across a continent? The detectives had not stuck to the trail so long. It was Friedman alone, apparently, who carried danger so close to Hagger time and again, and the yegg touched his side, where the comforting weight of the automatic pistol was suspended. For that, after all, seemed to be the only thing to settle Friedman's hash; he rather wished that he had sent home the shot when he had spotted the young man beside the lamppost.

"I'm getting sappy," said Hagger to his coffee. "I'm getting soft like a baby, by George."

He determined to leave the railroads, for, after all, it was not so extremely odd that he had been followed, even by an amateur detective, considering that he had stuck to the main arteries of traffic. A bit of chance and good luck might have kept Friedman up with him, but, now, he would put the jeweler to the test.

Hagger left Denver that same day and walked for fifteen hours with hardly a stop. The walk beat his feet to a pulpy soreness, but Hagger ever had a soul beyond the reach of physical pain, and he persisted grimly. He spent the night in a barn, and the next morning was picked up by a truck, carrying milk toward the nearest town. That brought him another twenty miles toward the nothingness of the open range, for it seemed like nothingness to Hagger's city-bred soul. His eyes were oppressed by the vastness of rough mountains, and the mountains themselves shrank small under the great arch of the sky.

To the illimitable reach of the sky itself he looked from time to time and shook his head, for the heavens that were familiar to him were little narrow strips of gray or blue running between the tops of high buildings. On an ocean trip one could escape from this lonely sense of bigness in the smoking salon or at the bar, but the loneliness was inescapable.

Vague tremors of fear, as inborn as the pangs of conscience, beset Hagger, for, if pursuit came up with him, what could he do? There was no crowd into which one could plunge, no network of lanes and alleys to receive a fugitive. He felt that he was observed from above as inescapably as by the eye of the moon, and who can get away from that, no matter how swiftly one runs?

He was lost. He was adrift in a sea of mountain and desert, only knowing indistinctly that Denver was a port behind and San Francisco a port ahead. He managed to steal rides on rickety trains that went pushing out like feeble hands into darkness, but so vast were the dimensions of this land that he felt as though he were laboring on a treadmill.

Much had to be done on foot. He bought a rifle, a stock of ammunition, a package of salt, cigarette tobacco, and a quantity of wheat-straw papers. In this manner he felt more secure in the wilderness, and although he found game scarce and rifle work very different from pistol play, yet he could get enough to live on.

He had one deep comfort—that Friedman was being left hopelessly behind. He laughed when he thought of that tall, frail youth attempting to match strides with him through such a wilderness as this where a day's journey advanced one hardly a step toward the goal.

Eventually, of course, he would come out on the farther side, and a few drinks and five minutes of the glare of city lights would take from his soul the ache of the wounds that it now was receiving. So he consoled himself.

Bitter weather began to come upon him. All deciduous trees were naked, and he passed small jungles of stripped brush encased in ice. Snow fell, and once the road turned to ice when a sleet storm poured suddenly out of the black heavens. Still, Hagger kept on. He did not laugh, but he was not disheartened—he had the patience of a sailor in the days of canvas voyaging toward almost legendary shores. He had to sleep outdoors, improvising some shelter against the weather.

Once, after walking all night, he had to rest for a whole day at a village; he swallowed a vast meal and then lay with closed eyes for hours. Here he bought a horse, saddle, and bridle. But he was ill at ease in a saddle. The unlucky brute put its foot in a gopher hole near the next crossroads town and broke its leg. Hagger shot it and carried the accouterments into town, where he sold them for what they would bring. After that, he trusted to his feet and the trains, when he could catch them. He spent as few hours as possible in towns, eating and leaving at once, or buying what he needed in a store and going on, for he knew that idle conversations mark a trail broad and black. He did not realize that his course was spectacular and strange, and that everyone would talk about a stranger who actually made a journey on foot and yet was not an Indian. He was living and acting according to his old knowledge, but he was in a new world of new men.

One day, as he was plodding up a grade toward a nest of bald-faced hills, a horseman trotted up behind him.

"Hagger, I want you," said a voice.

Hagger turned and saw a sad-faced man with long, drooping mustache looking at him down the barrel of a rifle.

"Tuck your hands up into the air," said the stranger.

"What d'you want me for?" asked Hagger.

"Nothin' much. I'm the sheriff, Hagger. You stick up your hands. We'll talk it over on the way to town."

Hagger smiled. There was a delicious irony of fate in this encounter, and he felt that there was laughter in the wind that leaped on him at that moment, carrying a dry flurry of snow. That flurry was like a winged ghost in the eyes of the sheriff's young horse, and it danced to one side, making him reach for the reins. Still holding his rifle in one hand, he covered Hagger, but the yegg asked no better chance than this. His numbed hand shot inside his coat; the rifle bullet jerked the hat from his head, but his own shot knocked the sheriff from his horse.

Hagger stopped long enough to see scarlet on the breast of the man of the law. "If you'd known Hagger, bud," he said, "you'd have brought your friends along, when you came after me."

Behind the saddle he found a small pack of food. He took it, and, leaving the groaning sheriff behind him, he went up the trail, contented.

At the top of the next hill he paused and looked back. The sheriff was feebly trying to sit up, and Hagger thought of retracing his way and putting a finishing bullet through the head of the man. However, it would waste time. Besides, the sheriff had his rifle and might fight effectively enough. So the yegg went on again, doggedly facing the wind.

The wind hung at the same point on the horizon for five days, growing stronger and colder, but Hagger accepted it without complaint. It bit him to the bone, but it acted as a compass and told him his direction. Twice he nearly froze during the night, but his marvelous vitality supported him, and he went on again and warmed himself with the labor of the trail.

It now led up and down over the roughest imaginable hills and mountains. All trees disappeared save hardy evergreens; the mountains looked black; the sun never shone, and all that was brilliant was the streaking of snow here and there.

Now and again he passed cattle, drifting aimlessly before the wind, or standing head down in the lee of a bluff, their stomachs tucked up against their backs, dying on their feet. So he did not lack for fresh meat.

Presently, however, his supplies ran out, and after that he pushed on through a nightmare of pain. He began to suffer pain in the stomach. Weakness brought blind spells of dizziness, in the midst of one of which he slipped and nearly rolled over the edge of a precipice. But it never occurred to him to pause or to turn back. Nothing could lie ahead much worse than what he had gone through.

Then, on the third day of his famine, he saw a hut, a squat, low form just visible up a narrow valley. He turned instantly toward it.

IV

Since the sheriff had known of him, everyone in this country might know, Hagger reflected. Therefore, he made a halt near the hut, and beat some warmth and strength into his blue hands. He looked to his automatic; the rifle slung at his back would probably be too slow for hand-to-hand work. After he had made these preparations, he marched on to the hut, ready to kill for the sake of food.

He knocked but got no answer. He knocked again, and this time he was answered by a shrill snarling. He called out. The dog inside growled again.

This pleased Hagger, for he realized that the owner of the place must have left and the dog was there to guard the shack until the return of his master. When that master returned, however, he would find something gone from his larder, and something more from his wardrobe.

The door was closed, but, oddly enough, it was latched from the outside. This puzzled Hagger for a moment, until he remembered that, of course, the master of the house would have secured the door from that side in leaving. So he set the latch up, and prepared to enter.

Inside, the dog was giving the most furious warning, and Hagger poised his automatic for a finishing shot. He could have laughed at the thought that any dog might keep him from making free with that heaven-sent haven.

Steadying himself, he jerked the door wide and poised the pistol.

A white bull terrier came at him across the floor in a fury, but plainly the dog was incapable of doing damage. The animal staggered, dragging his hind legs. His ribs thrust through his coat, and the clenched fist of a man could have been buried in his hollow flanks. Hagger kicked him. The terrier fell and lay senseless with a thin gash showing between his eyes where the toe of the boot had landed.

Then Hagger kicked the door to and went to find food. There was very little in that hut. On a high shelf behind the stove he found two cans of beans and pork, a half moldy sack of oatmeal, and the remnant of a side of bacon. There was coffee in another tin, some sugar and salt, and a few spices. That was all.

Hagger ate the sugar first in greedy mouthfuls. Then he ripped open a can of beans and devoured it. He was about to begin on the second, when the terrier, reviving, came savagely at him, feebler than before, but red-eyed with determination to battle.

Hagger, open can in hand, looked down with a grim smile at the little warrior. He, too, was a man of battle, but surely he would not have ventured his life for the sake of a master's property as this little fellow was determined to do.

"You sap," said Hagger, "a lot of thanks he'd give you. Why, kid, I'd be a better friend to you, most likely."

He side-stepped the clumsy rush of the fighting dog and saw the terrier topple over as it tried to turn.

"You'd show, too," said Hagger, nodding wisely, because he knew the points of this breed. "You'd show and win. In New York. At the Garden . . . is what I mean."

He stooped and caught the lean neck of the dog by the scruff, so that it was helpless to use its teeth. Then he spilled some beans on the floor before it.

"Eat 'em, you dummy," said Hagger, still grinning. "Eat 'em, Bare Bones."

The sight of food had a magic effect on the starved brute. Still, he did not touch it at once. His furious eyes glared suspiciously at Hagger. He was growling as he abased his head, but finally he tasted—and then the beans were gone. Gone from the second can of Hagger, too.

He went to a shed behind the house and found firewood corded there. He brought in a heaping armful and crashed it down. The stove was covered with rust, and, when the fire kindled, it steamed and gave out frightful odors. Hagger was unaware of them, for he was busy preparing the coffee, the oatmeal, and the bacon. Presently the air cleared, the fumes evaporated, and the warmth began to reach even the most distant corners of the cabin.

At length the meal was ready. Hagger piled everything on the little table and sat down to eat. He was half finished, when he was aware of the dog beside the table, sitting up with trembling legs, slavering with dreadful hunger, but with the fury gone from eyes that followed every movement of Hagger's hands, mutely hoping that some of the food would fall to its share.

It was not mere generosity that moved the man, rather, it was because his hunger was already nearly satisfied and he wished to see the terrier's joy at the sight of food. He dropped a scrap of bacon, and waited.

The dog shuddered with convulsive desire. His head ducked toward the scrap, and then he checked himself and sat back, watching the face of the stranger for permission. Hagger gaped, open-mouthed.

Faintly he sensed the cause. Having received food from his hand, the dog, therefore, looked upon him as a natural master, and, being a master, he must be scrupulously obeyed. Something in the heart of Hagger swelled with delight. Never had he owned a pet of any kind, and the only reason that bull terriers had a special interest for him was that he had seen them fighting in the pit.

"Take it, you little fool," said Hagger.

Instantly the morsel was gone. The tail beat a tattoo on the floor. "Well I'll be hanged," Hagger said, and grinned again.

When he offered the dog another bit in his hand, it was taken only after the word of permission, and the red tongue touched his fingers afterward in gratitude. Hagger snatched his hand away, looked at it in utter amazement, and then he grinned once more.

"Why, damn me," murmured Hagger. "Why, now damn me." He continued feeding the dog the bacon bit by bit. Suddenly: "You rascal, you've stole all my bacon!" cried Hagger suddenly.

The dog stood up, alert to know the man's will, tail acquiescently wagging, ears flattened in acknowledgment of the angry tone. Already there seemed more strength in the white body. Tenderness rose in the heart of Hagger at that, but he fought the unfamiliar feeling.

"Go in the corner and lie down," he commanded harshly.

The dog obeyed at once and lay in the farthest shadow, motionless, head raised, as though waiting for some command.

But warmth and sleepiness possessed Hagger. He flung himself down upon the bunk and slept heavily until the long night wore away and the icy dawn looked across the world. Then he awakened. He was very cold from head to foot, except for one warm spot at his side. It was the dog, curled up and sleeping there.

"Look here," said Hagger, sitting up. "You're a fresh sap to come up here, ain't you? Who invited you, dumbbell?"

The terrier licked the hand that was nearest him, then crawled up and tried to kiss the face of Hagger, masked in its bristling growth of many days.

The yegg regarded the dog with fresh interest.

"Nothing but blue ribbons," he said. "Nothing but firsts. Nothing but guts," he went on in a more emotional strain. "Nothing more but clean fighting. Why, you're a dog, kid."

The dog, sitting on the bunk, cocked its head to follow this language and seemed to grin in approval.

"So," said Hagger, "we're gonna get some breakfast, kid. You come and look."

He went out, carrying his rifle, and the terrier staggered to a little pool nearby and licked feverishly at the ice. When Hagger broke the heavy sheet, the animal drank long. There was less of a hollow within his flanks now. Turning from the little pond, Hagger saw a jack rabbit run from a bit of brush, followed by another a little smaller.

Luck was his. He dropped hastily to one knee and fired. The rearmost rabbit dropped; the other darted toward the safety of the shrubbery, but Hagger knocked him down on the verge of the shadows.

By the time he had picked up his first prize, the terrier was dragging the second toward him, but his strength was so slight that again and again he sprawled on the slippery snow.

Hagger strode back to the hut and from there looked toward the bushes. He could see that the dog had progressed hardly at all, but never for a moment did he relax his efforts to get the prize in.

V

The amusement of the yegg continued until he saw the dog reach the end of its strength and fall. Then he strode, still laughing, to the rescue, and picked up the rabbit. The terrier, panting, then managed to get to its feet and move uncertainly at the heels of its new master. Now Hagger built another roaring fire and roasted the larger of the rabbits. The second he fed to the dog while he ate his own portion. Then sleepiness came upon him the second time, for Nature was striving in her own way to repair the ravages of cold and starvation in him.

When he wakened, his nerves were no longer numb, his body was light, and strength had returned to his hands. He saw that he had slept from early morning until nearly noontide. So he hastened to the door and swept the horizon with an anxious glance. He hardly cared, however, what enemies awaited him, for now that he was himself once more, he felt that he could face the world with impunity. Indeed, he looked out on no human enemy, but upon a foe that would nevertheless have to be reckoned with. The wind that had blown steadily all these days had fallen away at last, and was replaced by a gentle breeze out of the south carrying vast loads of water vapor toward the frozen north. The water fell as huge flakes of snow, some of them square as the palm of a man's hand. Sometimes the air was streaked by ten million pencil lines of white wavering toward the earth, and sometimes the wind gathered strength and sent the billows uncertainly down the valley, picking the white robes from the upper slopes and flinging them on the floor of the ravine.

When he opened the door, it cut a swath in the heaped drift that had accumulated before the shack. Hagger stepped into the softness and whiteness with an oath. He saw nothing beautiful in the moth wings that were beating so softly upon the world, and he cursed deeply, steadily. "There's no luck," said Hagger. "Only the sneaks and the mollycoddles . . . they got all the luck. There ain't no luck for a man."

He was disturbed by something writhing within him, and, turning, he picked up the dog out of the drift where it was vainly struggling. The terrier was much stronger now. Still, his ribs stuck out as mournfully as ever, and his body was a mass of bumps and hollows. It would be days before strength really returned to him.

Hagger prepared himself at once for the march. His self-confidence rose proudly in spite of the labor that confronted him, and he felt his strength turn to iron and his resolution harden. In a way he loved peril and he loved great tasks, for what other living was there, compared with these crises when brain and soul had to merge in one flame or the labor could not be performed?

He had cleaned the cabin of its entire food cache, meager as it had been.

"If there was more than I could pack," declared Hagger to himself, "I'd burn it up . . . I'd chuck it out to spoil in the wet. Why, such a skunk as him, he don't deserve to have a bite left him . . . a low hound . . . that would leave a pup to starve . . . why, hell!" concluded Hagger.

This raised in Hagger an unusual sense of virtue. For by comparing himself with the unknown man who had left the white dog to the loneliness and starvation of this cabin he felt a surge of such self-appreciation as brought tears to his eyes. His breath came faster, and he reached for the terrier's head and patted it gently. The dog at once pressed closer to him and tried to rest its forepaws upon his knee, but it was far too weak and uncertain in its movements to manage such a maneuver.

It was time to depart, and Hagger walked to the door lightly and firmly.

"So long, old pal," said Hagger to the dog, and walked away.

The snow was still falling fast, sometimes heaving in the wind and washing like billows back and forth, so that it seemed wonderfully light and hardly worth considering. But in a few strides it began to ball about his feet and caused him to lift many extra pounds with either leg. Moreover, reaching through this white fluff, he had no idea what his footing would be, and repeatedly he slipped. He knew that he had left the narrow trail, and he also knew that it would be hopeless to try to recover it. All of this within the first fifty strides since he left the door of the shack.

Then he heard a half-stifled cry behind him, like the cry of a child. It was the white dog coming after him in a wavering course—sometimes he passed out of sight in the fluff. Sometimes his back alone was visible.

Hagger, black of brow, turned and picked up the dog by the neck. He carried him to the cabin, flung him roughly inside, and latched the door.

"Your boss'll come back for you," said Hagger.

He walked away, while one great wail rose from within the cabin. Then silence.

Straight up the valley went Hagger, regardless of trail now, knowing that he must reach the higher land at the farther end quickly, otherwise the whole ravine would be impassable, even to a man on snowshoes, for several days. He pointed his way to a cleft in the mountains, now and again visible through the white phantoms of the storm. The wind, rising fast, pressed against his back and helped him forward. He felt that luck was turning to him at last.

Yet, Hagger was dreadfully ill at ease, a weight was on his heart. Something wailed behind him.

"Your boss'll come back for you, you sap," said Hagger. Then he added with a shudder: "My God, it was only the wind that yelled then."

But he had lied to the dog and himself, for he knew that the man would not and could not come back, and, when he did, the terrier would be dead.

Hagger turned. The wind raged in his face, forbidding him. All his senses urged him to leave that fatal ravine. The wide, white wings of the storm flew ceaselessly against him. "You go to hell!" said Hagger with violence. "I'm gonna go back. I'm gonna . . ." He bent his head and started back.

It was hard going through the teeth of the storm, but he managed it with his bulldog strength. He came at last to the shack once more, a white image rather than a human being, and jerked open the door. Through the twilight he had a dim view of the terrier rising from the floor like a spirit from the tomb and coming silently toward him.

Hagger slammed the door behind him and stamped some of the snow from his boots. The heat of his body had melted enough of that snow to soak him to the skin. He felt a chill cutting at his heart, and doubly cold was it in the dark, moist hollow of that cabin. He would have taken a rock cave by preference. There was about it something that made him think of a tomb—he dared not carry that thought any further.

The brave and mighty Hagger sat for a long, long time in the gloom of this silent, man-made cave. In his lap lay the head of the dog, equally silent, but the glance of the man was fixed upon eternity, and the glance of the dog found all heaven in the face of the man.

At length Hagger roused himself, for he felt that inaction was rotting the strength of his spirit. Blindly he seized the broom that stood in a corner of the shack and swept furiously until some warmth returned to his spirit and his blood was flowing again. Then he stood erect in the center of the shack and looked around him.

Already, as he knew, the snow outside was too deep to admit his escape, and still it fell, beating its moth wings upon the little cabin. He was condemned to this house for he knew not how long, and in this house he must find his means of salvation.

Well, he had plenty of good seasoned wood in the shed behind the shanty—for that he could thank heaven. He had salt to season any meat he could catch and kill. And, besides, he was fortified by two enormous meals on which he could last for some days.

The dog, too, was beginning to show effects from the nourishment. Its eyes were brighter, and its tail no longer hung down like a limp plumb line. By the tail of a dog you often read his soul.

But Hagger avoided looking at the terrier. He feared that, if he did so, a vast rage would descend upon him. For the sake of this brute he had imperiled his life, and, if he glanced at the dog, he would be reminded that it was for the sake of a dumb beast that he had made this sacrifice which, in a way, was a sacrilege. For something ordained, did it not, that the beasts should serve man rather than man the beasts?

If such a fury came upon him, he would surely slay the thing that had drawn him back to his fate.

VI

For the salt and the fuel Hagger could give thanks. For the rifle, the revolver, the powder and lead he need offer no thanksgiving. He had brought them with him. With these he could maintain his existence, if only prey were led within his clutches. But first of all he must devise some means for venturing upon the snow sea.

There was not a sign of anything in the house. He remembered that some discarded odds and ends had been hanging from the rafters of the shed, and for this he started.

When he would have opened the door, a soft but strong arm opposed him, and, thrusting with all his might, he had his way, but a white tide burst in upon him and flooded all parts of the room. The wind had shifted and had heaped a vast drift against the door. He beat his way out.

Then he saw that he must proceed with patience. To that end, therefore, Hagger got from the interior of the cabin a broad scoop shovel that, no doubt, had served duty many a winter before. With it he attacked the snow masses and made them fly before him. He began to throw up a prodigious trench. The door of the shack lay at the bottom of a valley, so to speak, and now he could see that the entire roof of the house had been buried by the same drift. A gloomy suspicion came to him. He feared . . . He hardly dared to name his fear, but hastened back into the house and kindled a fire. At once the smoke rolled back and spread stiflingly through the place.

He went doggedly out, turning his head so as to avoid the sight of the dog. He climbed to the roof, which slanted so that he had difficulty in keeping a footing there, and, working busily with his shovel, he cleared the snow away.

The snowfall ceased. The bright stars came out, and their glance brought terrible cold upon the earth, much more dreadful than anything Hagger ever had endured before. He had known extremities of heat, but even the most raging sun did not possess this invisible, still-thrusting sword. Sometimes he felt as though his clothes had been plucked from his back, and as though he were a naked madman, toiling there. Numbness, too, began to overtake him, and a swimming mist, from time to time, rose over his brain and dimmed the cruel light of the stars. However, Hagger saw only one way out, and he went doggedly ahead. *Only a cur will quit. A dog shows his teeth to the end.* That was an old maxim with Hagger, who had seen the pit dogs die like that, grinning their rage, seeking gloriously for a death hold on the enemies before death unloosed their jaws.

So Hagger worked his way to the ridge of the roof. With some difficulty he cleared the chimney, and then descended to work on the fire. Bitter work was that. He laid the tinder and the wood, but, when he attempted to light a match, his cold-stiffened fingers refused to grip so small a thing. He tried to hold a match between his teeth and strike the bottom of the match box broadly across it. But he merely succeeded in breaking half a dozen. He went out into the starlight and shook the contents of the box into the palm of his hand.

There were three matches left. No, no! Not matches—but three possibilities of life, three gestures with which to defy the white death. Now, at last, the utter cold of fear engulfed the heart and the soul of Hagger and held him motionlessly in the night until something touched his leg.

He looked down and saw the raised head of the bull terrier. A new wonder gripped Hagger. After all, he was clad and the dog was thinly coated at best. He was in full strength, and the beast was a shambling skeleton. He was a man and could make his thoughts reach beyond his difficulties with hope, at least. He possessed strong hands, and so could labor toward deliverance. But the beast had none of these things, and, yet, he made not so much as a gesture of rebellion or doubt—not one whimper escaped from that iron heart of his. Silently he looked up to this man, this master, this god. Behold, his tail wagged, and Hagger was aware of a trust so vast that it exceeded the spirit of glorious man.

Hagger stumbled back into the cabin and fell on his knees. He did not pray. He merely had tripped on the threshold, but he found the dog before him, and he gathered that icy, dying body into his arms. He felt a tongue lick at his hands. "Christ . . . Christ," whispered Hagger, and crushed the dog against his breast. Perhaps that was a prayer, certainly it was not a curse, and who knows if the highest good comes from us by forethought or by the outbursting of instinct.

But after those two words had come chokingly from the throat of Hagger, warmth came to his breast from the body of the dog, and that warmth was a spiritual thing as well. Now he stood up, and, when he tried a match, it burst instantly into flame.

Hagger looked up—and then he touched the match to the tinder—flame struggled with smoke for a moment, as thought struggles with doubt, and then the fire rose, hissed in the wood, put forth its strength with a roar, and made the chimney sing and the stove tremble while Hagger sat broodingly close, drinking the heat and chafing on his knees the trembling dog.

At length he began to drowse, his head nodded, and he slept. How late he had labored into that night was told by the quick coming of the dawn, for surely he had not slept long when the day came. The stove was still warm, and the core of the red fire lived within the ashes. The dog was still slumbering in his arms.

Hagger woke. He roused the fire and began at the point where he had left off in the starlight. That is, under a sunny sky from which no warmth but brilliant light descended, he opened the rest of his way to the shed, and there he examined the things which, as his mind dimly remembered, had been hanging from the rafter. About such matters he knew very little, but, probably from a book or a picture, he recognized the frames of three snow-shoes and understood their uses—but to the frames not a vestige of the netting adhered.

When Hagger saw that he looked down to the dog at his side.

"Your skin would be what I need now," said Hagger. At this, the terrier looked up, and Hagger leaned and stroked its head, then he cast about to find what he could find. What he discovered would do very well—the half-moldy remnants of a saddle—and out of the sounder parts of the leather that covered it he cut the strips and fastened them onto the frames. It required all of a hungry day to perform this work, and, when the darkness came, his stomach was empty, indeed, and the belly of the dog clave to his back, for the terrible cold invaded the bodies of beast and man even when the fire roared close by—invaded them, and demanded rich nurture for the blood.

Hagger strapped the shoes on and went off to hunt. Since the dog could not follow, he was bidden to remain behind and guard. So, close to the door he lay down, remembering, and resistant even to the glowing warmth of the stove, with its piled fuel. Hagger went out beneath the stars.

The shoes were clumsy on his feet, particularly until he learned the trick of trailing them with a short, scuffling gait. The snow had compacted somewhat, still it was very loose, and it would give way beneath him and let him down into a cold, floundering depth now and again. In spite of this, he made no mean progress, working in a broad circle around the shack, until he came to windward of a forest where the snow had not gathered to such a depth in the trough of this narrow ravine, and where the going was easy enough.

Other creatures besides himself had found this favorable ground, for, as he brushed into a low thicket on the edge of the woods, a deer bounded out. Hagger could hardly believe his good fortune and brought the rifle readily to his shoulder. Swathed in rags and plunged into his coat pocket, he had kept his right hand warm, and the fingers were nimble enough as he closed them on the trigger. Yet the deer sped like an arrow from the string, and, at the shot, it merely leaped into the air and swerved to the side out of sight behind some brush.

Hagger leaped sideways to gain another view, another shot, and, so leaping, he forgot the snowshoes. The right one landed awkwardly aslant on the head of a shrub, twisted, and a hand of fire grasped his foot. He went down with a grunt, writhed a moment, and then leaned to make examination. The agony was great, but he moved the foot deliberately until he was sure that there was no break. He had sprained his ankle, however, and sprained it severely. And that was the end of his hunting. Perhaps the end of his life, also, unless help came this way.

VII

Quick help, too, was what he needed, for the cold closed on him with penetrating fingers the instant he was still. On the clumsy snowshoe he could not hop, and he saw at once what he must try to do. He took the shoes from his feet and put them on his hands. Then he began to walk forward, letting the whole weight of his body trail out behind.

It is not a difficult thing to describe, and even a child could do it for a little distance, whereas Hagger had the strength of a giant in his arms and hands. However, a hundred yards made him fall on his face, exhausted, and the cabin seemed no closer than at the beginning. When he had somewhat recovered, he began again. He discovered now that he could help a little by using his right knee and left leg to thrust him, fish-like, through the snow, but the first strength was gone from his arms. They were numb.

Yet he went on. When he came to the shed, it seemed to him that miles lay before him to the cabin, and, when he gained the cabin door, he looked up to the latch with despair, knowing that he never would have the strength to raise himself and reach it with his hand.

Yet, after some resting, the strength came. He opened the door, and the terrier fell on him in a frenzy of joy, but Hagger lay at full length, hardly breathing. The labor across the floor to the stove was a vast expedition. Once more he had to rest before he refreshed the dying fire, and then collapsed into a state of coma.

* * * * *

When the dawn came, Hagger had not wakened, but a loud noise at the door roused him, and, bracing himself on his hands, he sat up and beheld the entrance, with the dazzling white of the snow field behind him, a tall figure, wrapped in a great coat and wearing a cap with fur ear pieces. Snowshoes were on his feet, and his mittened hands leveled a steady rifle at Hagger.

"By the living damnation," said Hagger. "It's the jeweler."

"All I want," Friedman said calmly enough, "is the cash that you got from Steffans. Throw it out."

Hagger looked at him as from a vast distance. The matter of the jewel robbery was so faint and far off and so ridiculously unimportant in the light of other events that suddenly he could have laughed at a man who had crossed a continent and passed through varied torments in order to reclaim $7,000. What of himself, then, who had made the vaster effort to escape capture?

"Suppose I ain't got it?" he said.

"Then I'll kill you," said Friedman, "and search you afterward. Do you think I'm bluffing, when I say that, Hagger?"

He ended on a note of curious inquiry, and Hagger nodded.

"No, I know that you'd like to bash my brains out," he said without emotion. "How did you find out about Steffans and the amount of money . . . and everything?"

"I trailed you there, and then I made Steffans talk."

"You couldn't," said Hagger. "Steffans never talks. He'd rather die than talk."

"He talked," said the jeweler, smiling a little. "And now I've talked enough. I want to have that money and get out of here. If I stay much longer, I'll murder you, Hagger."

Hagger knew that the man meant what he said.

"Call off that dog!" said Friedman, his voice rising suddenly.

The terrier had crawled slowly forward on his belly. Now it rose and made a feeble rush at the enemy, for it appeared that he knew all about a rifle and what the pointing of it signified.

For one instant, Hagger was tempted to let the fighting dog go in. But he knew that the first bullet, in any case, would be for himself, and the second would surely end the life of the dog. He called sharply, and the dog pulled up short and then backed away, snarling savagely.

Hagger threw his wallet on the floor, and Friedman picked it up and dropped it into his pocket.

"You ain't even going to count it?" said Hagger.

"It's all you've got," said Friedman, "and how can I ask to get back more than you have. God knows what you've spent along the road." He said it in an agony of hate and malice; he said it through his teeth, as though he were speaking of blood and spirit rather than of hard cash.

"I spent damned little," said Hagger regretfully. "I wish that I'd blown the whole wad, though."

"Good-bye," said Friedman, and backed toward the door. "D'you sleep on the floor?"

Hagger could have laughed again, in spite of the agony from his foot—for exhaustion had made him fall asleep without removing his shoes, and now the swelling was pressing with a dreadful force against the leather. But he could have laughed to think that such enemies as he and his victim should talk in this desultory fashion, after the trail that each had covered. Those fellows who wrote the melodrama with the fine speeches, he would like to have a chance to tell a couple of them what he thought of them and their wares. This was in his mind, when he felt derisive laughter rising to his lips.

"Sure, I sleep on the floor," he said, "when I got an ankle sprained so bad that I can't move, hardly. Otherwise," he added savagely, "d'you think that you would have been able to get the drop on me so dead easy as all this? Say, Friedman, d'you think that?"

Friedman lingered at the door, taking careful stock of the thief. Hagger had no weapon at hand, therefore, he admitted carelessly: "It wouldn't have made much difference. I didn't have a bullet in the gun."

"You didn't what?"

The jeweler chuckled, and, throwing back the bolt, he exposed the empty chamber. "I lost the cartridges in the snow. I don't know much about guns," he declared.

Hagger was a little moved. After all, $7,000 in cash would not give him food in the cabin or heal his injured ankle. But again he was touched with calm admiration of the shopkeeper. "Friedman," he said, "did you ever do any police work? Ever have any training?"

"No. Why?"

"Well, nothing. Only you done a pretty fair job in getting at me here."

"When I heard about the way you'd shot the sheriff," said Friedman, "and nearly killed him, I just started in circles from that point. There wasn't anything hard about it."

"No?"

"It just took time."

"What did you live on through the storm?"

"Hardtack. I still got enough to bring me back to town." He took a square, half-chewed chunk of it from the pocket of his great coat. "And what did you live on, Hagger?"

The sublime simplicity of this man kept Hagger from answering for a moment, and then he said: "I found a little chuck in this shack . . . ate that . . . shot a couple of rabbits."

"What'll you live on now?"

"Hope, kid." Hagger grinned.

The jeweler scanned the cabin with a swift glance, making sure of the vacant shelves and the moldy, tomb-like emptiness of the place. Then a grin of savage joy transformed him suddenly, and he began to nod, as though an infinite understanding had come to him.

"It'll take a while," he said. "You'll last a bit. And maybe your ankle will get well first."

"Maybe," said Hagger.

"And maybe the man who owns this place'll come back."

"Maybe," said Hagger.

Friedman turned his head a little, looked over the banked snows, and then at the growing clouds on the southern sky. "No," he said with decision, "I guess not."

"Not?"

"I guess not. None of those things'll happen. This looks to me to be about the end of you, Hagger."

"Maybe," assented Hagger.

Friedman ginned again, with a sort of terrible, hungry joy.

"You wouldn't do a murder," said Hagger curiously.

"Me? No, I'm not a fool!"

"Well . . ." said Hagger, and left the rest of his thought unsaid.

He closed his eyes. When he opened them again, Friedman was outside the door.

"Hey, Friedman, Friedman!" called Hagger.

The man turned and leaned through the doorway. "There's no use whining and begging," he said. "You got no call on me. You got what's coming to you, and that's all. If I were in your place, *I* wouldn't whine."

"I want only one minute, Friedman."

"There's a storm coming. I can't wait."

"You'll rot in hell, Friedman, if you don't listen to me."

"Go on, then," said Friedman, leaning against one side of the door. "I'll listen."

"It's about the dog," said Hagger.

VIII

At this the eyes of the jeweler narrowed a little. One could see disbelief in them, but he merely grumbled: "Make it short, will you? What're you driving at, Hagger?"

"This dog, here, you take a look at him. You got a liking for dogs, Friedman, I guess?"

"Me?" said Friedman. "Why should I like the beasts?"

Hagger stared. "All right, all right," he said. "You don't like 'em, but this is a special kind of a dog. You know what kind, I guess?"

"A white dog," Friedman said, only interested in that he was waiting for some surprise in the speech of the yegg.

"A bull terrier," said Hagger violently. "These here . . . they're the only dogs worthwhile. These are the kings of the dogs. Like a gent I heard say . . . 'What will my bull terrier do? He'll do anything that any other dog'll do, and then he'll kill the other dog.'" Hagger laughed. It was a joke that he appreciated greatly.

But Friedman did not even smile. "Are you killing time?" he asked at length.

"All right," said Hagger, shrugging his shoulders. "Only what I really want to tell you is this . . . this dog'll stick by you to the limit. This dog'll die for you, Friedman."

"He looks more like he'd tear my throat out. But, look here, Hagger, what sort of crazy talk is this? Why should I give a damn about a dog, will you tell me that?"

"You don't," said Hagger slowly as he strove to rally his thoughts and find a new turning point through which he could gain an advantage in this argument. "You don't. No, you're a damned intelligent, high type of man. You wouldn't have been able to run me down, otherwise. And you want a good practical reason, Friedman. Well, I'll give you one. You take that dog out to civilization, and you put him up for sale, what would you get?"

"Get? I dunno. Twenty-five dollars from some fool that wanted that kind of a dog."

"Yeah?" sneered Hagger. "Twenty-five dollars, you say? Twenty-five dollars!" He laughed hoarsely.

The jeweler, intrigued, knitted his brows and waited. "Maybe fifty?"

"Five hundred!" said Hagger fiercely.

Friedman blinked. "Go on, Hagger," he said. "You're trying to put something over on me."

"Am I? Am I trying to put something over on you? You know what the best thoroughbred bull terriers fetch, when they're champions, I suppose?"

"Is this a champion?" asked Friedman.

"He is," lied Hagger with enthusiasm.

"Champion of what?"

"Champion bull terrier of the world!" cried Hagger.

"Well," said Friedman. "I dunno . . . this sounds like a funny yarn to me."

"Funny?" cried Hagger, growing more enthusiastically committed to his prevarications. "Funny? Look here, Friedman, you don't mean to stand up there and tell me man to man that you really don't know who this dog is?"

"How should I know?" asked Friedman.

"Well, his picture has been in the papers enough," said Hagger. "He's had interviews, like a murderer or a movie star, or something like that. He's had write-ups and pictures taken of him. I'll tell you who he is. He's Lambury Rex . . . that's who he is!"

This fictitious name had a great effect upon the listener, who displayed a new interest.

"It seems to me that I've heard that name," he said. "Lambury Rex? I'm pretty sure that I have."

"Everybody in the world has," Hagger assured him dryly. "I said that he was worth five hundred. Why, any first-rate bull terrier is worth that. Five hundred! A man would be a fool to take twenty-five hundred for a dog like this. Think of him taking the first prize . . . finest dog in the show . . . a blue ribbon . . ."

"Did he do that?"

"Ain't I telling you? Say, Friedman, what have I got to gain by telling you all this?"

"I dunno," Friedman assured him, "and I see you're killing time, because what does it matter about the dog?"

"You poor fool!" shouted Hagger. "You poor sap! I'm offering you this dog to take out of the valley with you. Does that mean anything, you square head?"

Friedman said nothing for a moment and then growled: "Where do you come off in this?"

"Listen!" shrieked Hagger. "Why do I have to come off in it? Why? I offer you a dog! Talk sense, Friedman. Here's something for nothing. Here's the finest dog in the world . . ."

Friedman cut in coldly: "And you're offering him to me?"

"I see," Hagger said slowly, nodding. "Why should I give him to you, when you've been trailing me, and all that. Well, I've got no grudge against you. I soaked you for seven thousand. You soaked me and got it back. We're all square. But the main thing is this . . . Friedman, don't you leave this dog behind to starve here in the shack with me."

"Maybe he won't die of starvation," said Friedman. "Maybe he'll make a couple of meals for you first. Stewed dog for Hagger?" He laughed cynically, but his laughter died at once, stopped by the expression of unutterable contempt and disgust on the face of the yegg.

"Anyway," said Hagger, "that's the end of your joke. Take him, Friedman. Take him along and make a little fortune out of him. Or keep him and he'll get you famous."

"Look here," said Friedman. "How could I ever get him through the snow?"

"You broke a trail to come in," said Hagger. "You could take him back the same way. He's game. He'll work hard. And . . . and you could sort of give him a hand now and then, old fellow."

Hagger was pleading with all his might. He had cast pretense aside, and his heart was in his voice.

"It beats me," Friedman said suddenly. He stepped back inside the shack. He sat down in one of the chairs and regarded the yegg closely—his twisted foot and his tormented face. "It beats me," repeated Friedman. "You, Hagger, you're gonna die, man. You're gonna die, and yet you're talking about a dog."

"Why," said Hagger, controlling his temper, "will it do me any good to see a dog starve at the same time that I do?"

"Might be company for you, I should think . . . since you like the cur such a lot."

"Cur?" said Hagger with a terrible frown. "Damn you, Friedman, you don't deserve to have a chance at the saving of a fine animal like him, a king of dogs like Linkton Rex . . ."

"A minute ago," cut in the jeweler sharply, "you called him Lambury Rex."

"Did I? A slip of the tongue. You take me, when I get excited, I never get the words right and . . ."

"Sure you don't." The visitor grinned, wide and slow. "I don't believe this dog is worth anything. You're just trying to make a fool of me. It'd make you die happier, if you could laugh at me a couple of times while you're lying here. Ain't that the truth?"

The yegg suddenly lay back, his head supported by the wall of the shack. Now his strength had gone from him for the moment, and he could only look at Friedman with dull, lackluster eyes.

Vaguely he observed the differences between himself and the jeweler, measured the narrow shoulders, the slender hands and feet, the long, lean face, now hollowed and stricken by the privations through which the man had passed. Weak physically, he might be, but not of feeble character. He had sufficient force and determination to trail and catch up with Hagger himself—once Hagger had been detained by the dog.

"I tell you," said Hagger, "it's fate that you should have the terrier. If it hadn't been for him, you never would have caught me, Friedman."

"Wouldn't I?" said Friedman. His head was thrust out, like the head of a bird of prey. "I would have followed you around the world."

"Until you were bashed in the face!" said the yegg savagely.

"No, it was the will of God," said the jeweler, and piously he looked up.

Hagger gaped. "God?" he said. "What has God got to do with you and me?"

"He stopped you with a dog, and then He made me take you with an empty gun. It's all the work of God."

"Well," said Hagger slowly, "I dunno. I don't seem to think. Only I know this . . . if you ain't gonna take the dog away with you, then get out of here and leave me alone, will you? Because I hate the sight of your ugly mug, Friedman. I hate you, you swine!"

Friedman, on his clumsy snowshoes, backed to the door and hesitated. Twice he laid his hand upon the knob. Twice he hesitated and turned back once more. Then with sudden violence he sat down in the chair again.

Hagger screamed in hysterical hatred and rage: "Are you gonna get out of here, Friedman? If I get my hands on you, you'll die before me, you and your cash! Friedman . . . what are you doing?"

The question was asked in a changed voice, for Friedman was unlacing the lashes of his own snowshoes.

IX

"What d'ya mean? What d'ya mean?" cried the yegg. "What're you taking off your snowshoes for?"

Friedman stood up, freed from the cumbersome shoes, and eyed Hagger without kindness. "Lemme see your foot," he said, "and stop your yapping, will you?"

To the bewilderment of Hagger, Friedman actually trusted himself within gripping distance of his powerful, blunt-fingered hands that could have fastened upon him as fatally as the talons of an eagle. Regardless, apparently, of this danger, Friedman kneeled at his feet and began to cut the shoe with a sharp knife, slicing the leather with the greatest care, until the shoe came away in two parts. The sock followed. Then he looked at the foot. It was misshapen, purple-streaked, and the instant the pressure of the shoe was removed, it began to swell.

Friedman regarded it with a shudder, and then looked up at the set face of Hagger. "I dunno . . . I dunno . . ." said Friedman, overwhelmed. "You talked dog to me, with this going on all the time . . . I dunno . . ." He seemed quite shaken. "Wait a minute," he said.

Now that the shoe was off, instead of giving Hagger relief, the pain became tenfold worse, and the inflamed flesh, as it swelled, seemed to be torn with hot tongs. He lay half sick with pain.

Now Friedman poured water into a pot and made the fire rage until the water was steaming briskly. After that, he managed hot compresses for the swelling ankle, and alternately chilled the hurt with snow and then bathed it in hot water, until the pain of the remedy seemed far greater than the pain of the hurt.

Then Friedman desisted and sat back to consider his task. The moment he paused, he was aware of the howling of the wind. Going to the door, he pushed it open a crack and saw that the storm was coming over the ravine blacker than ever, with the wind piling the snow higher and higher. He slammed the door, then turned with a scowl on his companion.

"Well," said Hagger, "I know how you feel. I feel the same way. It's hell . . . and believe me, Friedman, you never would've caught me, if it hadn't been for the dog."

"If it hadn't been for the dog, I'd've been out of the valley before the storm came," declared Friedman bitterly. "It's got the evil eye, that cur." He scowled on the white bull terrier, then he sat down as before, like an evil bird, his back humped, his thin head thrust out before him. "What do you eat?"

"Snow," said the yegg bitterly.

"Well?"

"There's deer around here . . . sloughs of 'em. I potted one last night, and it was the side jump I took to see what come of it that done me in like this." He added: "I got an idea that maybe you could get a deer for us, Friedman. For yourself and me and the dog is what I mean, y'understand?"

"I understand."

"Well?"

"I couldn't hit a deer."

"You can when you have to. If you couldn't hit a deer, how can you expect to hit me?"

"I know. That's bad. Well," agreed Friedman, "I'll go out and call the deer, Hagger. Maybe I could hit it, then." Armed with Hagger's automatic, Friedman went to the door. "Maybe the dog could go along?" he suggested, and snapped his fingers and clucked invitingly.

The answer of the terrier was a snarl.

"Seems to hate me," said Friedman. "Why?"

"I dunno, just a streak of meanness in him, most likely."

The touch of sarcasm in this answer made Friedman draw his thick brows together. However, the next instant he had turned again to the door.

"Head for the forest right down the ravine and bear left of that," said Hagger. "That's where I found a deer . . . maybe you'll find 'em using the same place for cover."

Friedman disappeared.

His sulkiness filled Hagger with dismay, and, shaking his fist at the dog, he exclaimed: "You're scratching the ground right from under your feet, pup! We never may see his ugly mug again!"

Meantime, he was much more comfortable. The rigorous and patient treatment given to his injured ankle had been most effective. Now blood circulated rapidly in the ankle—there was no quicker way in which it could be healed.

The dog, undismayed by the shaken hand, pricked his ears and crowded close to his master, and Hagger lay back, comforted, smiling. He let an arm fall loosely across the back of Lambury Rex and chuckled. How long would it take Friedman to come to this intimate understanding with the animal?

Indeed, Friedman might never enter that door again. Hagger himself in such a case never would come back to the cabin, housing as it did only a man and a dog. The wind still was strong, and the snow still fell. Again and again a crashing against the walls of the cabin told how the bits of flying snow crust were cutting at the wood. They would cut at a man equally well, and no one but a sentimental fool, Hagger told himself, would have done anything but turn his back to that wind and let it help him out of the valley.

In the course of the next hour he guessed that Friedman never would come back, and from that moment the roar of the storm outside and the whistling of the wind in the chimney had a different meaning. They were the dirges for his death. Calmly he began to make up his mind. As soon as the wood that now filled the stove had burned down, he would kill himself and the dog. It was the only manly thing to do, for, otherwise, there was only slow starvation before them.

Suddenly the door was pushed open, and Friedman stood in the entrance. In the faint dusk that dimly illumined the storm outside he seemed a strong spirit striding through confusion. On his back there was a sight almost as welcome as himself, a shoulder of venison of ample proportions.

"It was the deer you shot at," said Friedman, putting down his burden and grinning as the dog came to sniff at it. "I found it lying just about where you must have put your slug into it. It was almost buried in the snow."

"Did it take you all this time to walk there and back?" asked the yegg.

"No," replied Friedman slowly, "it wasn't that. When I first got out and faced the wind, it seemed to blow the ideas out of my mind. I figured that it was best just to drift with the wind right out of the ravine. And I had gone quite a long distance, when there was a howling in the wind . . ."

"Ah?" said Hagger, stiffening a little.

"A sort of wailing, Hagger, if you know what I mean . . ."

"Yes," said Hagger. "I know what you thought, too."

"No, you couldn't guess in a million years, because I never had such a thought before. I ain't a dreamer."

"You thought," said Hagger, "that it was the wail of the dog, howling behind you. Sort of his ghost, or something, complaining."

Friedman bit his lip anxiously. "Are you a mind-reader?" he asked.

"No, no," said Hagger, "but, when I started to leave the valley, I heard the same thing, and I had to come back. Maybe, Friedman," he added in a terrible whisper, "maybe, Friedman, this here dog ain't just what he seems . . . but . . ."

"Cut out the spooky stuff, will you?" snarled Friedman. "How could a dog do anything like that?"

"I dunno," said Hagger, "but suppose that . . . well, let it go. Only he never seemed like any other dog to me, and no other dog could do to you what he's done."

"You talk like a fool," said Friedman, his anger suddenly flaring.

"Who's the biggest fool?" sneered Hagger. "You'd have to ask the dog."

X

The ankle grew strong again. It should have kept Hagger helpless for a month, but, by the end of a fortnight of constant attention, he could walk on it with a limp, and it was high time for him to move. The weather that had piled the little ravine with snow had altered in a single day; a Chinook melted away the snow and filled the little creek with thundering waters from the mountains. The haze and the laziness of spring covered the earth and filled the air. It would be muddy going, but go they must—Friedman back to his shop in far-away Manhattan, and Hagger to wherever fate led him on his wild way.

On the last night they sat at the crazy table with a pine torch to give them light and played cards, using a pack they had found forgotten in a corner. They played with never a word. Speech had grown less and less frequent during the past fortnight. Certainly there was no background of good feeling between them, and all this time they had lived with an ever-present cause for dispute sharing the cabin with them. That cause now lay near the stove, stretched out at ease, turning his head from time to time from the face of one master to the other—watching them with a quiet happiness.

The dog was no longer the shambling, trembling thing of bones and weakness that first had snarled at the yegg. Now, sleek and glistening, he looked what Hagger had named him—a king of his kind. Two weeks of a meat diet were under his belt—all that he could eat, and days of work and sport, following through the snow on those hunts that never failed to send Friedman home with game, for the ravine had caught the wildlife like a pocket, the deep, soft snows kept it helpless there, and even the uncertain hand of Friedman could not help but send a bullet to the mark—had made the dog wax keen and strong.

Now and again, briefly and aslant, the two men cast a glance at the white beauty, and every time there was a softening of his eyes and a wagging of his tail. But those looks seldom came the dog's way. For the most part the pair eyed one another sullenly, and the silent game of cards went on until Friedman, throwing down his hand after a deal, said: "Well, Hagger, what about it?"

It was a rough, burly voice that broke from the throat of Friedman, but then the jeweler was no longer what he had been. The beard made his narrow face seem broader, and the hunts and exercise in the pure mountain air had straightened his rounded shoulders. Hagger met this appeal with a shrug of his shoulders, and answered not a word, so that Friedman, angered, exclaimed again: "I say, what about the dog . . . tomorrow?"

The keen eyes of Hagger gathered to points of light. For a moment the men stared at one another, and not a word was said. Then, as though by a common agreement, they left their chairs and turned in for the night.

The white dog slept on the floor midway, exactly, between the two.

* * * * *

Dawn came, and two hollow-eyed men stood up and faced one another—Friedman keenly defiant and Hagger with gloomy resolution in his face.

He jerked his head toward the bull terrier. "He and me . . . we'd both be dead ones," said Hagger, "except for you. You take him along, will you?"

Such joy came into the face of Friedman as nothing ever had brought there before. He made a quick gesture with both hands as though he were about to grasp the prize and flee with it. However, he straightened again. As they stood at the door of the shack, he said briefly, his face partly averted: "Let the dog pick his man. So long, Hagger."

"Good-bye, Friedman."

Each knew that never again would he be so close to the other.

They left the doorway then, Friedman turning east, for he could afford to return through the towns, but Hagger faced west, for there still was a trail to be buried by him.

And behind Friedman trotted the bull terrier. The sight of this, from the tail of his eye, made Hagger reach for his automatic. He checked his hand and shook his head, as so often of late he had shaken it, bull-like, when the pains of body or of soul tormented him.

Every day, when Friedman went out to hunt, the terrier, after that first day of all, had trailed at his heels. Habit might have accounted for choice now, but to Hagger that never occurred. In a black mist he limped forward, reaching once and again for his gun, but thinking better of it each time.

He heard a yelping behind him, and, glancing back, he saw that the terrier was circling wildly about Friedman and catching him by a trouser leg, starting to drag him back in the direction of Hagger.

Friedman would not turn. Resolutely, head bent a little, he went up the wind through the ravine as if nothing in the world lay behind him—nothing worthy of a man's interest.

Then a white flash went across the space between the two. It was the dog, and, pausing midway, he howled long and dismally, as if he saw the moon rising in the black of the sky.

There was no turning back, no pleading from Friedman, however, but, as though he knew that the dog was lost to him, suddenly he threw out his hands and began to run. Running, indeed, to put behind him the thing that he had lost.

Hagger faced forward. There was happiness in his heart, and yet, when the white flash reached him and leaped up in welcome, he was true to his contract, as Friedman had been, and said not a word to lure the terrier to him. There was no need. Behind his heels, the dog settled to a contented trot, and, when after another hour of trudging Hagger paused and sat on a rock to rest his ankle, the terrier came and put his head upon his master's knee.

All the weariness of the long trail, and all the pain of the last weeks vanished from the memory of Hagger. He was content.

XI

He killed two rabbits and a pair of squirrels that day. Never had his aim been better, not even when he spent a couple of hours each day tearing the targets to bits on the small ranges in New York. He and the terrier had a good meal, and that night the dog curled up close to his master and slept.

Hagger wakened once or twice. He was cold in spite of the bed of fir branches that he had built, and the warmth of the dog's body. But he was vastly content, and, putting forth his hand, he touched the white terrier softly—and saw the tail wag even in the dog's sleep. He had the cherishing feeling of a father for a child.

When he wakened in the early dawn, he turned matters gravely in his mind. He could go back to the great cities for which he hungered, where crowds were his shelter, and whose swarms made the shadow in which he retreated from danger. But how should he get to any such retreat with the dog? How could the dog ride the rods? How could the dog leap on the blind baggage?

For some reason that he could not understand, but which was simply that the dog had chosen him, he was forced to choose the dog. It was vain for him to try to dodge the issue and tell himself that he was meant for the life of the great metropolitan centers. The fact that was first to be faced was the future of the dog. He decided, therefore, that he would take time and try to settle this matter by degrees, letting some solution come of itself.

For two days he wandered and lived on the country, and then he saw before him a long, low-built house standing in a hollow. He looked earnestly at it. There he could possibly find work. The mountain range and its winter lay whitening behind him, shutting off his trail until the real spring should come, and, in the meantime, should he not stop here and try to recruit his strength and his purse? Little could be accomplished without hard cash. So he felt, and went on toward the ranch house.

There were the usual corrals, haystacks, sheds, and great barns around the place. It looked almost like a clumsily built village, in a way. So he came up to it with a good deal of confidence. Where so many lived, one more could be employed.

He met a bent-backed man riding an old horse.

"Where's the boss?"

"G'wan to the house. He's there, of course."

He went on to the house and tapped at the door. A Negro came to the door.

"Where's the boss?"

"Whatcha want with 'im?"

"Work."

"Well . . . I dunno . . . I'll see. What can ya do?"

"Anything."

The Negro grinned. "That's a long order," he said, and disappeared.

At length, a young man stepped from the house and looked Hagger in the eye.

"You can do anything?" asked the rancher.

"Pretty near."

"A good hand with a rope, then, of course."

"A which?" said Hagger.

"And, of course, you can cut and brand?"

"What?"

"You've never done any of those things?"

"No," said Hagger honestly, beginning to be irritated.

"Have you ever pitched hay?"

Hagger was silent.

"Have you ever chopped wood?"

Hagger was silent still.

"You'd be pretty useful on a ranch." The rancher smiled. "That's quite a dog," he added, and whistled to the bull terrier.

The latter sprang close to Hagger and showed his teeth at the stranger.

"A one-man dog," said the rancher, and he smiled as though he approved. "How old is he?" he asked at length.

"Old enough to do his share of killing."

"And you?" asked the rancher, turning with sudden and sharp scrutiny on Hagger.

Again Hagger was silent, but this time his eyes did not drop. They fixed themselves upon the face of the rancher.

The latter nodded again, slowly and thoughtfully.

"I can give work, and gladly," he said, "to any strong man who is willing to try. Are you willing to try?"

"I am," said Hagger.

"To do anything?"

"Yes."

"And your dog, here . . . I have some very valuable sheep dogs on the place. Suppose that he meets them . . . is he apt to kill one of 'em?"

Hagger stared, but he answered honestly: "I don't know."

At that there was a little silence, and then the rancher continued in a lowered voice: "I have some expert hands working on this place, and they have a great value for me. Suppose you had some trouble with them . . . would you . . . ?" He paused.

After all, there was no need that the interval should be filled in for Hagger, and he said slowly and sullenly: "I don't know."

The dog, worried by his master's tone, came hastily before him and, jumping up, busily licked his hands.

"Get down, you fool!" said Hagger in a terrible voice.

"*Hmmm*," said the rancher. "The dog seems fond of you."

"I got no time to stand here and chatter," said Hagger, reaching the limit of his patience. "What can I do? I don't know. I ain't weak. I can try. Rope? Cut and brand? I dunno what you mean. But I can try."

The rancher looked not at the man but at the dog. "There must be something in you," he said, "and, if you're willing to try, I'll take you on. You go over to the bunkhouse and pick out some bunk that isn't taken. Then tell the cook that you're ready to eat. I suppose you are?"

"I might," said Hagger.

"And . . . what sort of a gun do you pack?"

"A straight-shooting one," said the yegg, and he brought out his automatic with a swift and easy gesture.

The rancher marked the gun, the gesture, and the man. "All right," he said. "Sometimes a little poison is a tonic. I'll take you on."

So Hagger departed toward the bunkhouse.

* * * * *

It was much later in that same day—when Hagger had finished blistering his hands with an axe. At that time the wife of the rancher returned from a canter across the hills and joined her husband in his library, where he sat surrounded by stacked paper, for he was making out checks to pay bills.

"Richard!" she said.

"What's happened, dear?"

"How did that dreadful man come on the place? He has a face like a nightmare!"

"Where?"

"You can see him through the window . . . and . . . good heavens! . . . Dickie and Betty are with him! Your own children . . . and with such a brute as that! I want him discharged at . . ."

"Hush," said Richard. "Don't be silly, my dear. Look at the man again."

"I've looked at him enough. He makes me dizzy with fear."

"Does a master know a servant as well as a servant knows the master?"

"What on earth are you talking about?"

"Well, my dear, when you look at the man, look at the dog."

It was a busy and tangled bit of play in which Hagger was employed in an apparent assault upon the son of the family, and, although Dickie was laughing uproariously with the fun, the white bull terrier had evidently a different view of the matter, for, taking his master by the trousers, he was attempting with all his might to pull him away from mischief.

"What a blessed puppy," said the wife.

"Aye," said the rancher, "there's more in dogs than we think."

Red Fire

This final installment of the four-part saga of Paul Torridon, a character known as White Thunder among the Cheyennes, was originally published in the June 30, 1928 issue of Street & Smith's *Western Story Magazine* under Faust's Peter Henry Morland byline. Each installment is able to stand alone and yet, taken together, they comprise a coherent narrative. The first part, "Torridon," can be found in *Gunman's Rendezvous* (Skyhorse Publishing, 2015); the second, "The Man from the Sky," in *Peyton* (Skyhorse Publishing, 2015); and the third, "Prairie Pawn," in *The Steel Box* (Skyhorse Publishing, 2015).

I

It was a small band of buffalo, an offscouring or little side eddy from one of the black masses of millions that moved across the plains, and, when Rushing Wind came on their traces, his heart leaped with the lust for fresh meat. Parched corn and dried buffalo flesh, tasteless as dry chips of wood, had been his diet for days during a lonely excursion upon the prairie. He had gone out from the Cheyenne village like some knight of the olden days, riding aimlessly, praying for adventure, hoping greedily for scalps and for coups to be counted. But no good fortune had come his way. For ten days, patient as a hungry wolf, he had dogged the way of a caravan of white men, pushing west and west, but he had had no luck. In the night they guarded their circle of wagons with the most scrupulous care. In the day, their hunting parties were never less than three well-armed men. And though their plains craft might not be of a very high order, it was an old maxim among the Cheyennes that all white men shoot straight with a rifle. The Indians were apt to attribute it to bigger medicine. As a matter of fact, it was simply that the whites had infinitely more powder and ball to use in practice. The red man had to get his practice out of actual hunting or battle. Accordingly Rushing Wind had at last turned off from the way of the caravan and struck at a tangent from its line across the prairie, and now he had come upon the trail of the buffalo.

When he first came on the trail, he leaned from the saddle and studied the prints. The grass was beginning to curl up and straighten again around the marks of the hoofs. So he knew that the animals had passed within a few hours. He set off after them cautiously, creeping up to the top of every swale of ground.

It was a typical plains day, bright, warm, and so crystal-clear that the horizon line seemed ruled in ink. Presently he saw the moving forms far off. They were drifting and grazing to the south. The wind lay in the southeast. Therefore, he threw a long, loose circle to the north and west, coming up cautiously in the shelter of some slightly rising ground.

Coming to the crest, he dismounted, and lay flat in the tall grass. This he parted before his face and looked out. He was very close to them. There was a magnificent bull. He admired the huge front, the lofty shoulders of the animal, but he knew that the flesh of such an experienced monster would be rank to the taste and so tough that teeth hardly could manage it—not even such white, strong teeth as armed the mouth of this Cheyenne. Then he slid backward through the grass.

As he did so, a second rider to the rear, a man on a silver-flashing gray mare, dismounted and sank into the grass, and his horse sank down with him.

Rushing Wind sat up and looked all around him, as though some shadow of danger had swept across his mind, like the dark of a cloud across the ground. It was not fear of immediate danger, however. It was merely the usual caution of a wild thing hunting in the wilderness, and, therefore, in constant dread of being hunted. For just as he had wandered across the plains in search of adventure and scalps and coups and plunder, so many another individual was cruising about the prairies, as keen as he, as crafty, as clever with weapons, as merciless.

Seeing nothing between him and the horizon, however, the young Cheyenne returned to his patient horse and took from the case strapped behind his saddle a strong war bow made of the toughest horn of the mountain sheep, boiled, straightened, and then glued and bound together in strips. It was flexible enough to stand infinite bending and yet stiff enough to require all the weight of a strong man's shoulder to draw an arrow home against such resistance.

He had a long and heavy rifle as well, but, as usual, he was abroad with a most scanty supply of the precious powder and lead. He had to save that for human enemies. He strung the bow with some difficulty, tried the strength of the beautifully made cord by drawing it to his shoulder several times, and then selected from the quiver several hunting arrows—that is, arrows that having been shot into game could be drawn forth, and the head, at least, used again and again. The arrows for war, of which he had an additional small supply, were barbed so that it would be a murderous task to draw them from the flesh.

When he had made sure that the bow was in good condition and the arrows all that he desired, he planted in the ground his long lance, hung his shield upon it, with the festoon of eagle feathers hanging from its face, and then carefully leaned the invaluable rifle against this stand. Next he loosed the packs from behind the saddle of the pony.

It might be that the chase would be long. In any case, the pony needed all its agility in the dangerous task that lay before it. After that, he stood before the head of the horse and looked keenly into its eyes.

They were like the eyes of a beast of prey—bright, treacherous, wild. But the Indian looked for no softness and kindness there. He would have been suspicious of a friendly glance. What he wanted was what he found—untamable fierceness, endurance, force of heart.

Assured of this, he bounded into the saddle and began to work the pony around the edge of the hill with much caution, for the buffalo sometimes seemed to be endowed with an extra sense that told them of approaching danger.

In fact, as he rounded the hill, he saw the entire little herd rushing off at full speed, their hoofs clacking sharply together, the ground trembling under the beat of their heavy striding.

He was after them with a yell. Heavy and cumbersome as the buffalo looks, he can run at a good pace, and he can maintain it through a wonderful length of time. It takes a good horse to come up with them, but the pony that this young brave bestrode was the best of his herd, and his own herd was a hand-picked lot.

Like an antelope it flashed forward. It passed a lumbering yearling. It ranged beside a three-year-old cow. Then the bow was at work at once. Drawn to the shoulder, it drove a shaft with wonderful force. At four hundred yards a Cheyenne bow had been known to strike game and to kill it. And if Rushing Wind was an archer not quite up to such a mark as this, at least he sent the shaft into the side of the cow behind the shoulder almost up to the feathers.

The big animal swerved, coughed, and then dropped upon its knees, skidding forward through the grass.

That was food for the Cheyenne. His sport was still ahead of him, and with a yell he sent the pony forward. The bull ran well, but there was still a burst of sprinting left in the horse. It carried its master straight up to the panting bull, and a second arrow went from the bow. This time it struck dense bull hide. It sank deep in the flesh of the big fellow, but the roll of muscles and the looseness of the skin itself forced the arrow upward. The bull was merely stung, and he whirled toward the rider with such suddenness that the second arrow that flew from the string merely ripped a furrow in the tough back of the buffalo.

With a roar came the bull, a veteran of many a battle with his kind and ready to fight once more against such a strange foe. The surge of its head swept past the flank of the pony narrowly as the active little horse bounded to the side.

Presenting his battle front, circling as the Indian circled, the bull waited, tearing up the ground, sending his long, strange bellow booming, so that it seemed to be flooding up from the earth itself and rising now here, now there.

Rushing Wind, his eyes on fire, began to maneuver the little pony like a dancer, but it was some moments before the foaming horse caused the bull make a false step that left the tender flank open again. Then loudly twanged the bow string, and the arrow sank into the side of the monster half the length of the shaft.

The bull charged, but blindly. He came to a halt, tossing his head. His hide twitched convulsively, so that the two arrows imbedded in him jerked back and forth. His head lowered. Blood burst from his mouth. He sank to his knees, and even then, with more courage than strength, he strove to rise, and still he boomed his defiance. Life was passing from him quickly, however. Before the last of his fleeing herd was out of sight, he rolled upon his side, dead.

From the carcass, the Cheyenne took only the tongue. He returned to the cow, took from her the tongue, also, and then prepared to remove some other choice bits. He would gorge himself in a great feast, dry the flesh that remained in strips, and then set himself for the homeward journey. It was not a great thing to have killed two buffalo, but it was better than nothing, and it was, perhaps, the explanation of the dream that had sent him forth to try his fortune in the open country alone. At least, he had not so much as broken the shaft of an arrow in this encounter. The arrows, soon cleaned and restored to his quiver, were as good as ever, though they might be the better for a little sharpening.

On the whole, the heart of Rushing Wind was high, and he returned cheerfully to the point where he had left his other weapons, hastening a little on his still sweating horse, because he was as anxious about the welfare of the rifle as though it were a favorite child.

He sighed with relief when he found that lance and shield and rifle and pack were all in place, and, dismounting, he looked first to the gun, stroking it with a smile. It was half weapon and half medicine, in the eyes of Rushing Wind. He had only one thing more precious, and that was the richly ornamented hunting knife in his belt, the gift of that prince of doctors and medicine men, White Thunder.

Something stirred just behind the Indian. It was no more than the slightest of whispers in the grass, but it made the young Cheyenne twist sharply around.

He found a white hunter risen to his knees in the grass, a long rifle at his shoulder, and a deadly aim taken upon his own heart.

"Stand fast," said the white man. "Drop your rifle. You still may live to return to your lodge."

He spoke in fairly good Cheyenne, and the young brave said with a groan: "Roger Lincoln!" Clumsily the English words came upon his tongue. "And the dream was a lying dream that was sent to me."

II

In the first place, Rushing Wind was disarmed. Some brush grew nearby, hardly ankle high. Then, at the suggestion of the white man, they gathered some of this brush. They made a fire and began to roast bits of the tender buffalo tongues on the ends of twigs. While they cooked, they talked, the Cheyenne with a rising heart.

Roger Lincoln said in the beginning: "You were with Standing Bull when he came to Fort Kendry and first stole away Paul Torridon, who you call White Thunder?"

"I was not," said the Cheyenne.

"But you were with Standing Bull when he came up again and captured the white girl, Nancy Brett, and took her away across the plains?"

The young Indian raised his head and was silent. His eyes grew a little larger, as though he were in expectation of an outburst of enmity. But Roger Lincoln pointed to the little fire that was burning so cheerfully.

"We are cooking food together. When we eat together we are friends, Rushing Wind, are we not?"

The other hesitated: "It was I who was with Standing Bull," he said. "Why should I deny it? You saw me with him. I was with him when you offered all the guns and horses if he would set White Thunder free."

"But he would not do that."

"How could Standing Bull promise? How could any of us promise? Not even High Wolf, the greatest of our chiefs, could send him away. The people would not endure to see him go. They know what he has done for us."

Roger Lincoln nodded and frowned. "He has made rain for you, and through him you've killed a good many Dakotas."

"And he has healed the sick and given good luck to the men on the warpath. He brings the buffalo to the side of the village," added Rushing Wind.

"Those things have happened now and then. He doesn't do them every day."

"A man cannot hope to take scalps every day of his life," said Rushing Wind naïvely. "And," he added, growing sadder, "I never have taken a single one."

"All is in the hands of Heammawihio," said the white man. "All that a warrior can do is to be brave and ready. Heammawihio sends the good fortune and the bad. Tell me, are you a friend of White Thunder in the camp?"

The eye of the youth brightened. He took from his belt the hunting knife with the gaudy handle. Roger Lincoln had not troubled to remove that means of attack from his captive, as though he knew that his own great name and fame would be sufficient to keep the youngster from attacking hand to hand.

"This," said the young Cheyenne, "was given to me by White Thunder. You may judge if he is my friend."

"And Standing Bull. He also is your friend?"

"He is a friend to White Thunder. Not to me. Standing Bull," went on the boy carefully, "is a great chief." He explained still further: "White Thunder has made him great."

"No," said Lincoln. "Any man who dared to come into the middle of Fort Kendry twice and steal away whites is great without any help. But although this man is a great chief, he is not a great friend of yours?"

The boy was silent.

"Very well," said Roger Lincoln. "We cannot be friends with everyone. That isn't to be expected. But now I want you to look at everything with my eyes."

"I shall try," said the boy. "You are a great hunter of bears and buffalo . . . and men." He let his brow darken a little as he said this.

"Tell me," said Roger Lincoln. "Before White Thunder was stolen away, was I not a friend to the Cheyennes?"

"It is true," said the boy.

"He is my best of companions and friends," said Roger Lincoln. "Once my life lay at his feet like this fire at ours. He could have let it be stamped out, but he would not do that. He saved my life. And at that time I was a stranger to him. I was large and he was small. I was strong and he was weak. Now, after he had done that much for me, I ask you to tell me if he should not be my friend?"

The Cheyenne listened to this story with glistening eyes. "It is true," he said, and his harsh voice became soft and pleasant.

"However, he was stolen away by Standing Bull, whose life also White Thunder had saved," continued Roger Lincoln.

"Yes," said Rushing Wind, "and more than his life, his spirit."

"And after he was taken away, what should I do? Should I sit in my lodge and fold my hands?"

"No," Rushing Wind replied carefully. "You should have put on the war paint and gone on the warpath. And you have done it," he added. A glitter came in his eyes. "Six Cheyennes have died. Their names are gone. Their souls have rotted with their bodies on the prairies." He looked keenly at Roger Lincoln. "I am the seventh man," he said.

"You are not," replied the great hunter. "We eat together, side-by-side. I give you my friendship."

Rushing Wind replied, still hesitant: "The hawk and the eagle never fly side-by-side."

"Listen to me, hear with my ears and believe with my mind. In my day I have killed warriors. The list of them is not short. It would be a small pleasure to me to add one more man to the number who have gone stumbling before me to the house of darkness. But you can do a great service to me out of good will and with your life still yours."

The Cheyenne was silent, but obviously he was listening with all his might to this novel suggestion.

"I cannot buy your good will," said Roger Lincoln, "but I give your life back to you as a peace offering. This thing I will do, and I promise that I shall not take my gift back. Besides this, I ask no promise in return from you. I shall tell you the thing that I wish to do. Afterward, you will think. Perhaps you will wish to do what I want. Perhaps you will merely smile and laugh to yourself and say that I have talked like a fool."

He made a pause and began to eat heartily of the roasted tongue. The Cheyenne imitated that good example, and though he was a smaller man by far than Roger Lincoln, and though the white man had fasted the longer of the two, yet the Indian fairly ate two pounds for the one of his captor.

127

At last, Roger Lincoln pushed back a little from the fire. He filled a short-stemmed pipe and began to smoke strong tobacco. The Indian, however, took out a bowl of red catlinite, which he filled with a mixture, always holding the stem up as he worked. Then he lighted the tobacco and flavoring herbs with a coal from the little dying fire and began to smoke, after first blowing, as it were, libations to the spirit world.

Neither of them spoke until after a few minutes. Then Roger Lincoln said: "How did the girl come to the village?"

"She was very tired."

"Was she taken to the teepee of White Thunder?"

"Yes."

"How did he receive her?"

"In his arms. He . . ." The Cheyenne paused. And Roger Lincoln was silent, frowning with a desperate blackness at the sky before him.

"He received her, also," said Rushing Wind, "with tears."

His face was actually puckered with emotion as he said this. Plainly he could hardly connect the word tears with the word man and control his disgust. A flicker of contempt went over the face of Roger Lincoln, also. Men told their stories of how Roger Lincoln, on a time, had been tormented almost to death by a party of Crows, and how he had laughed at them and reviled them with scorn, heedless of his pain, until he was rescued by the luckiest of chances. So, being such a man as he was, he could not help that touch of scorn appearing in his face. However, he came instantly to the defense of his absent friend.

"No man can have all the strength in the world," he said.

"It is true," said the Cheyenne earnestly. "I would not have White Thunder think that I have spoken with scorn about him."

He glanced upward with awe and trouble in his face, as though he feared that a circling buzzard far above them might be an emissary sent by the medicine man to spy upon his words.

"However," said the Cheyenne, "everything is as I have told you. She began to wake up and hold out her arms to him. She was tired but happy."

"So," said the hunter. Then he kept silence, being deep in thought. At last he went on in a changed and gruffer voice: "He took her into his teepee?"

"Yes."

"He has kept her there ever since?"

"Yes."

Roger Lincoln exclaimed with something between disgust, impatience, and anger: "Then he has taken her as his wife, as an Indian takes a wife?"

At this, the Cheyenne shook his head.

"Who is to understand the ways of people who are guided by the spirits and the Sky People?" he said naïvely. "I, at least, cannot understand them."

"Why do you say that?"

"It is a big lodge," said the young warrior. "There is no whiter or finer lodge in all the camp of the Cheyennes. And now one part of it is walled off with curtains of deer skin from another part. And when they sleep, the girl goes into one side as though it were a separate lodge, and White Thunder goes into another part."

The light reappeared in the eye of Roger Lincoln. "A good lad!" he exclaimed. "I had written him down a good lad. I would have wagered my blood on him."

"Ha?" grunted Rushing Wind. "Then is this a mystery which you, also, understand?"

III

They stared for a moment at one another. But, since it was not the first time in the life of either that he had been aware of the great difference and distinction between the viewpoint of red man and white, they passed on in their conversation, Roger Lincoln taking the lead.

"The girl is now happy?" he asked. "Or does she sit and weep?"

"Weep?" said the Indian. "Why should a woman weep when she has become the squaw of a great medicine man such as White Thunder? No, she is singing and laughing all day long."

The white man smiled a little.

"Besides," said the Cheyenne, "she does little work. Her hands are not as big as my two fingers. Young Willow still keeps the lodge for White Thunder."

"And what of White Thunder himself? Is he happy, also?"

"He is more happy than he was," said the boy. "He is able to ride out now on the great black horse."

"Is he free, then?"

"Yes. He is not guarded except when the girl rides out with him. But when she is left behind in the lodge, the chiefs know that he will not go far."

"How far does he go?"

"Sometimes he is gone in the morning and when he comes back in the evening even the black horse is tired."

"There is no other horse like that one," admitted Roger Lincoln. "Though there was a time when I thought that Comanche was the swiftest foot on the prairie." He pointed to her and she, hearing her name and marking the gesture, came forward fearlessly, gently toward her master.

"It is plain that White Thunder put a spirit in her when he had her," said Rushing Wind. "She also understands man talk, as the black horse does."

"Does the black horse understand man talk?" queried Roger Lincoln, suppressing a smile.

"Perfectly," said the Cheyenne in all seriousness. "So well does the stallion understand, that he repeated to his master what the herd boys said to one another when they were out watching the horse." He began to fill his pipe again, observing the same careful formula as before.

"Ah, then," said Roger Lincoln, "people must be careful of what they say in front of this clever horse."

"As much so," replied the Cheyenne, "as if it were his master that listened. The tall brave with the scarred face, Walking Horse, said when he was near the big stallion that he thought White Thunder was a coward and not a good man. Not a week later Walking Horse's son fell sick and would have died. But Walking Horse took the boy and went to the lodge of White Thunder. He confessed his fault and asked for pardon, and begged White Thunder not to take away the life of his boy. So White Thunder kept the boy in his own lodge and made big medicine, and in a few days the boy could run home. Then Walking Horse gave White Thunder many good robes, and ten fine horses from his herd."

"By this I see," said Roger Lincoln, "that my good friend, White Thunder, is growing rich."

"He would be," replied the young brave, "the richest man who ever walked or rode among the Cheyennes. But what is wealth to him? It runs through his fingers. He gives to the poor of the tribe. He mounts the poor warriors from his horse herd and lets them keep the horses. His lodge is open to the hungry. What is wealth to him? He can ask more from the Sky People if there should be need."

This speech he made with perfect simplicity and openness of manner, and Roger Lincoln, watching narrowly, nodded his head.

"But still White Thunder is not happy?" he said.

"It is true that often he looks toward the horizon," was the answer.

"Then let me speak the truth. Has this medicine man great power?"

"That we all have seen."

"Has he struck down even the Dakotas with his wisdom?"

"And they turn aside, now, from our war trails," said the youth with a smile of savage triumph. "They are familiar with the medicine of White Thunder, and they do not wish to anger him again. They have not tried to strike us since the last battle. Even Spotted Antelope cannot find braves to follow him south against our lodges. They know that the birds of White Thunder would watch them coming."

"Do the birds work for White Thunder, then?"

"Yes. Do you see that buzzard still hanging in the sky above us?"

"Perhaps he is waiting until we go, so that he can drop down on the dead buffalo, yonder?"

"Perhaps," said the boy, but his smile showed that he was confident in his superior knowledge.

"Farther," he expanded suddenly, "than they can smell dead meat, the buzzards and all the other birds can hear the name of White Thunder, and they come to listen, and to talk to him."

"It is a great power," Roger Lincoln said, keeping a grave face.

"I myself," said the youth, "have seen a sparrow fly out from the lodge entrance of White Thunder."

Roger Lincoln, after this crushing proof, remained respectfully silent for some time. "Now tell me," he said finally, "if he has this great power, and if he is not happy among the Cheyennes, what keeps him from one day striking a great blow against the Cheyennes?"

"We are his people," said the boy uneasily. "He was sent to us. Standing Bull brought him."

"Did not White Thunder once ride away from you?"

"That is true," admitted the Cheyenne.

"May not White Thunder be waiting patiently, hoping that because of the great services he has rendered to your people they will soon set him free, and let him go, with many horses to carry him and his possessions over the prairie?"

The young warrior was silent, scowling at the thought.

"And when he finds that the thing is not done, may he not lose his patience at last? May he not strike down the whole village with sickness, and while they die, he will ride away?"

Rushing Wind opened his eyes very wide.

And, striking while the iron was hot, Roger Lincoln continued: "Now I shall tell you why my rifle did not strike you today. A dream came to me. My friend, White Thunder, stood before me and said . . . 'Every day I say to High Wolf and the other Cheyennes that I wish to be gone. They will not listen. Therefore, come and tell them for me. They may believe you. They are like children. They do not think that I shall strike them. Tell them. They may believe your tongue when they will not believe mine.'"

He paused, and Rushing Wind sat tense with fear and excitement.

"If I live to reach the village, I shall carry the word to High Wolf," the young Cheyenne said.

"That would be the act of a very young man," said Roger Lincoln.

"What should I do?"

"If you tell the chiefs, they will sit and do a great deal of talking with the old men. Everybody will talk."

"That is true." The young warrior nodded. "A great many words . . . many feasts . . . and nothing is done."

"At last they will not be able to give up White Thunder," Lincoln said. "He is precious to them. A man does not like to sacrifice his best rifle."

"True," said the Cheyenne again, wincing as he let his gaze rest upon his beloved weapon.

"And White Thunder is like a rifle to the Cheyennes."

"Then what should I do?"

"Be a brave and bold man, for your own sake, for your friendship to White Thunder, for the sake of your whole tribe . . . and for the sake, perhaps, of the life that I have given back to you this day."

Rushing Wind listened to this solemn prologue with grave, bright eyes.

"The day will soon come when you will be a guard with White Thunder in your care."

"True," said the youth.

"Let him ride out with the girl. Let him ride straight north. I, night and day, shall be waiting and watching for his coming. I shall have fast horses with me. It will be your part to handle the guards so that the two have a chance to get a little start. You are a strong young brave. Perhaps you will be the chief of the guards on that day."

"Perhaps," said the boy, stern and tense with excitement.

"Your own horse could stumble in the hunt. The other two or three you could first have sent back a little distance for some purpose. You could fire your rifle, and the bullet could miss the mark. These things all are possible."

"Among the Cheyennes," said Rushing Wind, "after that day I would be counted less than a dog in worth."

"You could leave the Cheyennes and come to us. We would make you richer than any chief."

"I would be known as a traitor. My tribe would scorn me."

"Time darkens the mind and the memory. After a little while you could come back. You would have fine horses and guns to give to the chiefs. You would have splendid knives, and horse loads of weapons and ammunition. You would make the whole tribe so happy with your return and the riches that you gave away that they would never raise a voice against you in the council."

Rushing Wind drew a great breath. His eyes were dim. The adventure was taking shape before them.

"And if you were not condemned in the council, you would be able to meet the warriors who spoke to you with anger or with scorn."

The breast of the youngster heaved with pride and with courage.

"But if you do not do this thing, no one will do it. I have been led by the dream to find you. The medicine of White Thunder is working already. It has brought me here. It fills your own heart, now. His bird is watching above us to listen to your answer. Tell me, Rushing Wind, will you deliver your people from danger, or will you not?"

Rushing Wind leaped to his feet and threw his hands above his head. "I shall!" he cried.

"Look," said the other. "The bird has heard. He departs to carry the news to his master."

For the waiting buzzard, which rapidly had been circling lower, now, startled as the Indian sprang up, slid away through the air, rising higher, and aiming straight south and east.

Young Rushing Wind stared after it with open mouth of wonder. "Great is the medicine of White Thunder," he said. "I am in his hands."

IV

When Rushing Wind returned to the Cheyenne camp, he wrapped himself in as much dignity as he could, because his expedition had not been successful. Not that this was a matter to bring any disgrace upon him. As a matter of fact, nine-tenths of the excursions—particularly the single-handed ones—never brought any results. But they were valuable and were always encouraged by the chief. No one was more valuable during the hardships of a long march than the young man who had learned to support himself for many days, weeks, or months, riding solitary on the plains. He who had made several of these inland voyages was looked up to almost as though he had taken a scalp or counted a coup. A chief gathering a party for the warpath was sure to try to include as many of these hardy adventurers as possible.

As he crossed the river, he saw some boys swimming. They spied him at once and came for him like young greyhounds, whooping. Around him they circled, rattling questions, but when they gathered from his silence and the absence of any spoils that he had not done anything noteworthy, they left him at once, scampering back to the water. For the day was hot, the air windless. Only one careless voice called over a shoulder: "You have come back in good time, Rushing Wind. Your father is dying!"

Rushing Wind twisted about in his saddle. Then he galloped furiously for the village, quite forgetting his dignity in his fear and his grief.

He passed like a whirlwind through the village. Vaguely he noted what lay about him. Rising Hawk had a new and larger lodge than ever. Waiting River, in front of his teepee, was doing a war dance all by himself, looking very like a strutting turkey cock. In front of the home of Little Eagle seven horses were tied, and Little Eagle was looking them over with care. Ah, Little Eagle had a marriageable daughter, and no doubt this was the marriage price offered by her lover.

Here, however, was his father's lodge. He flung himself from his pony.

Smoke issued in thin breaths from the entrance; he smelled the fragrance of the burning needles of ground pine, and knew that some doctor must be purifying the teepee.

Softly he entered.

There were no fewer than four doctors and their women at work in the lodge. They were walking back and forth or standing over the sick man, shaking the rattles of buffalo skin filled with stones to drive away the evil spirit that caused the sickness. As for Black Beaver, he lay stiffly on his bed, his face thin, cadaverous. His eyes were half opened. They looked to Rushing Wind like the eyes of a dead man.

Along the walls of the tent he saw his mother and the other squaw, watching with strained eyes, already gathering in their hearts, apparently, the fury of the death wail and the horror of the death lament.

Rushing Wind was a bold young brave, but he trembled with weakness and with disgust. Death seemed to him a foul, unclean thing. Such a death as this was most horrible. But a death in the open field, in battle—it was that for which a man was made.

He passed quickly through the weaving mass of the doctors and their women and crouched beside the bed of his father. So dense were the fumes of the sweet grass and the other purifying smokes that he hardly could make out the features of the warrior. He had to wave that smoke aside.

When his son spoke, Black Beaver merely rolled his eyes. His skin was dry and shining. It was hot as fire to the touch. Plainly he was out of his mind and very close indeed to death.

Rushing Wind himself felt dizzy and weak. He thought that it was the evil spirit of sickness coming out of his father's body and attacking him in turn. So he shrank back beside his mother. It was frightfully hot in the teepee. Naturally everything was closed to keep in the purifying smoke, and the fire blazed strongly. Outside, the strong sun was pouring down its full might upon the lodge.

"How long?" he asked his mother in the sign language.

"For three weeks," she said in the same method of communication.

"What has been done for him?"

"Everything that the wise men could do. Look now. You would not think that an evil spirit could stay in the body of a warrior when so much purifying smoke is in the air."

"No. It is wonderful." The boy sighed. "It must be a spirit of terrible strength. What was done at the first?"

"All that should be done. Your father began to tremble with cold one night. Then he burned with fever. He was nauseated. The next day he began to take long sweat baths, and after each bath he would plunge into the river. This he did every day."

"That was good," said the boy.

"Of course it was good. But he seemed to get worse. We called in a doctor. Still he got worse. Two doctors came. Now we have given away almost everything. There are only two horses left of the entire herd."

In spite of himself, Rushing Wind groaned. However, he was no miser. He said at once: "Why have you not called for White Thunder?"

"I would have called him. But your father and his other wife, here, would not have him. Your father does not like his white skin and his strange ways."

"Mother," said the boy, "I will go for him now. Black Beaver is wandering in his mind. He would not know what was happening to him."

"It is no use," said the squaw. "We have nothing to pay to White Thunder."

"But he often works for nothing."

"Your father is not a beggar, Rushing Wind," she answered.

"He will come for my sake. You will see that he will come gladly. He is my friend."

"There is no use," repeated the squaw sadly. "I have seen men die before. Your father is rushing toward the spirits. He will leave us soon. Nothing can keep him back, now."

Rushing Wind, however, started up and left the tent. When he stood outside the flap of the entrance and had carefully closed it behind him, he was so dizzy that he had to pause a moment before the clearer air made his head easier. It was marvelous, he thought, that such clouds of purification should not have cured his father.

He went at a run across the camp and came quickly to the lodge of White Thunder, noticeable from afar for its loftiness and for the snowy sheen of the skins of which it was composed. But when he stood close to the entrance, he heard voices and paused. He had seen a great deal of White Thunder, and the great medicine man always had been simple and kind to him. However, one never could tell. These men of mystery were apt to be changeable. Suppose that when he asked the help of the great doctor the latter demanded a price and then learned that only two horses remained to the sick man.

With shame and pride, Rushing Wind flushed crimson. He knew not what to do, so he hesitated.

"Here," the complaining voice of Young Willow was saying, "the red beads should go in a line that turns here."

"I shall do it over again," said the voice of Nancy Brett.

The brave listened with some wonder. The white girl had learned to speak good Cheyenne with marvelous speed. But, for that matter, of course the medicine of White Thunder would account for much greater marvels than this.

"Let the moccasins be," said White Thunder, yawning.

There was a cry of anger from Young Willow. "Do you want to teach your squaw to be lazy?" she asked.

"She is not my squaw," said White Thunder.

"Ha!" said Young Willow. "The stubborn man will not see the truth. It pleases him to be wrong because he prefers to be different. Is she not living in your lodge? Does she not eat your food? Does she not wear the clothes that you give her?"

"She is not my squaw," White Thunder persisted carelessly. "She is a stolen woman. Who asked her father for her? Who paid horses to her father?"

"What horses is she worth?" asked the squaw roughly.

"Hush," White Thunder said. "You are rude, Young Willow."

"I am not rude," said the old woman. "I love her, too. But she is a baby. I speak with only one tongue. I cannot lie. How many horses is she worth? She cannot do beadwork except slowly and stupidly. She cannot flesh a hide . . . her wrists begin to ache. She cannot tan deerskins. She does not know how to make a lodge or even how to put it up. She cannot make arrows."

"She is a wonderful cook," said White Thunder.

There was a peal of cheerful laughter. It fell on the ear of Rushing Wind like the music of small bells. He knew that it was the white girl laughing, and he wondered at her good nature.

"*Bah!*" said Young Willow. "What is a bow good for when it has only one string? Besides, marriage is more than a giving of horses. It is love, and you both love one another."

"Are you sure?" White Thunder asked.

"Of course I am sure," said the squaw. "You look at each other like two calves that have only one cow for a mother. I understand about such things. I am old, but I am a woman, too." She cackled as she said it.

"You are old," said a heavy voice—and Rushing Wind recognized the accents of Standing Bull, that battle leader—"you are old, and you are a fool. Old age is often a troublesome guest."

"If I am troublesome," grumbled Young Willow, "I shall go back to the lodge of my husband. I never have any thanks for the work that I do here."

"Do what you are bidden," rumbled Standing Bull. "Keep peace. Speak when you are bidden to speak. A woman's tongue grows too loose when she is old."

There was a cry of anger from Young Willow. "Why are you here to teach me?" she demanded of Standing Bull. "Go back to your own lodge. You have wives and you have children. Why do you always sit here? Why do you come here and look at this white girl like a horse looking at the edge of the sky?"

"I shall go," Standing Bull said with a grunt of anger.

"Stay where you are," said White Thunder. "When Young Willow is angry, her talk is like the throwing of knives. Don't pay any attention to it. We never do."

"I am going to get some wood," said Young Willow. "But today I have said something that a wise man would remember."

She came hurrying from the lodge, and behind her was the laughter of White Thunder. Rushing Wind prepared to enter.

V

He found on entering that White Thunder and the girl were still chuckling over the departure of Young Willow in a rage, while Standing Bull sat impassively in the place of honor in the lodge, propped luxuriously against a backrest, his gaze fixed upon vacancy.

It came to the mind of Rushing Wind that there might be much in the warning that had just been given to White Thunder by the squaw, but both the girl and the white man seemed oblivious of any such thought. Rushing Wind greeted all within the house with ceremony. He was given a place. Nancy Brett, smiling as a hostess should, offered him meat from the great pot in the center of the teepee, and he ate of it, as in duty bound. Then a pipe was passed to him and he accepted it, after White Thunder had lit it. Standing Bull inquired after the fortune of the young brave in the prairie, and the latter said simply: "I saw many days of riding, and many days of prairie, and many days of blue sky. But I found nothing but buffalo."

"Long journeys make good warriors," said Standing Bull sententiously. "I, before long, if the medicine is good, will start against the Crows. I shall remember you, Rushing Wind."

The young brave heard with eyes that sparkled. He was working his way up through the crowd of the younger warriors. Such a patron as White Thunder—and now the kindness of Standing Bull—promised him a future to which the doors stood wide.

"Now," said White Thunder, "you are very welcome to us, Rushing Wind. But is there any special reason why you have come to me?"

"My father is sick," said the young Cheyenne sadly. "It must be a very strong spirit that is harming him, because now there are ten rattles being shaken in his lodge, and still he grows sicker and sicker."

White Thunder rose at once. "Come," he said. "I shall go with you. I heard that your father would not have me near him. Otherwise, I should have offered to help long before."

"His mind is gone now," said the son, "and his eyes are in the other world. He cannot help but let you treat him."

They came to the lodge and at the entrance flap the steam and heat and smoke from the interior boiled out into the face of

Torridon. Inside, there was a wild tangle of figures, dancing in a crazy maze, raising a dust that thickened the haze, and chanting a howling dirge in unison.

"Listen," said the son in admiration. "Is it not wonderful that all this medicine cannot make my father well?"

Torridon stepped back from the lodge. "Send those rascals away," he said, flushing with anger. "Send them scampering. Clear every one of them out of the lodge. Then I will come in."

Rushing Wind was in desperate woe at this request. He was fairly overcome with anguish at the thought that he might offend one of the great doctors now at work in the lodge.

He said eagerly to Torridon: "If one gun is good, two guns are better . . . if one doctor is good, two doctors are better."

Torridon was too excited and angry to listen to this reasonable protest. He exclaimed again: "Send them out, Rushing Wind, or I'll turn my back on your lodge! Send them out. I'll tell you this much . . . they're killing your father as surely as if they were firing bullets into him."

Rushing Wind rolled his eyes wildly. But at length he hurried into the lodge and after a few moments the doctors began to issue forth, each puffing with his late efforts, each followed by a woman loaded down with rattles and animal masks, and other contraptions. They strode off, all turning baleful eyes upon Torridon as they went by. He had offended them before merely by the greatness of his superior medicine. But now he had interfered directly with their business, and they would never forget it, as he well knew.

He was in a gloomy state as he entered the lodge. Life in the Cheyenne community was dangerous enough already, but the professional hatred of these clever rascals would make it doubly so.

The women were on their feet when he came in, looking at him with doubt, awe, and fear in their eyes. He crossed at once to the sick man and saw that he was at death's door. Most mightily, then, did Torridon wish that he possessed some real knowledge of medicine. Instead, he had only common sense to fall back upon to save this dying man.

He ordered Rushing Wind and the squaws to roll up the sides of the lodge and to open the entrance flap. There was a groan in response. The air, they told him, was fairly rich and reeking with purifications and charms. All these were now to be dissipated. All these high-priced favors were to be blown away.

He was adamant. The tent was opened and fresher wind blew the foulness away. Yet it was very hot. The sun was relentless. The breeze hardly stirred. Torridon made up his mind at once.

"The underwater spirits," he said to Rushing Wind, "might help me to carry away the evil spirit that is in your father. He must be carried at once to the side of the river. Put two backrests together and then we will carry him. Let the women come after. They should bring robes, food, and plenty of skins to put up a little tent. Let this be done quickly."

It was done quickly, with many frantic glances at the man of the lodge, as though they feared the veteran warrior would give up the ghost at any moment. Rushing Wind took the head of the litter. Torridon took the feet—and light enough was their burden. For the fever had wasted poor Black Beaver until he was a ghost of his powerful self.

They bore him from the camp and then up the river to a considerable distance, so that the merry sounds of the boys at the swimming pool floated only dimly to their ears, like the broken songs of birds. Here Torridon chose a place high on the bank between two lofty trees. The tent was put up with speed and skill. Cut branches made the foundation on which the bed was laid, and Black Beaver was made warm and comfortable.

He had begun to roll his head from side to side and mutter. Sometimes the muttering rose to a harsh shout.

"He is dying," the younger squaw said, and fell on her knees beside the bed.

"Peace," said Torridon, who was reasonably sure that she was right. "The underwater spirits are now trying to take the evil out of him. That is why he shouts and turns. Because there is a battle going on in his heart."

He next asked what had been eaten by Black Beaver, and was told that for three days the warrior had refused everything, even the tenderest bits of roasted venison.

No wonder he was failing rapidly—a three-day fast, a burning fever, and a lodge choked with foul air and smoke!

Torridon had a broth cooked for the sick man. Then the head of Black Beaver was supported, and the broth poured down his throat. In the end the brave lay back with a groan. His eyes closed. Torridon thought that death actually had come. Silence fell on the watching group. But presently all could see that the sick man's breast was rising and falling gently.

"That is good," whispered Rushing Wind. "He sleeps. Oh, White Thunder, how mighty is your medicine. The others are nothing. All the other doctors are the rattling of dead leaves. You, alone, have power."

Torridon sat down, cross-legged, under a tree and looked at the hushed squaws, at the tense face of Rushing Wind, and wondered at himself. All his amateur attempts at cures had been strangely successful. Those powerful frames of the Indians, toughened by a constant life in the open, seemed to need nothing but a quiet chance and no disturbance in order to fight off every ill that flesh is heir to. The torments of the doctors, felt Torridon, had killed more than unassisted disease could have done.

He looked farther off at the prairie, wide as the sea and more level, no bush, no tree breaking its monotonous outline, and he wondered whether, when he returned to his own kind— if that ever was to be—he could accomplish among them work half so successful as that which he had managed among these red children. Among them he was a great man, he was a great spirit walking the earth by special permission of the Sky

People. Among his white cousins he would be insignificant Paul Torridon once more.

So he wondered, half sadly and half with resignation. He could see that his affairs were now involved in so great a tangle that his own volition was not sufficient to straighten matters out. Nancy Brett was in his hands. That situation could not continue. Vaguely he hoped that a priest might be found, somewhere, who would be brought to the camp to perform a marriage ceremony. Until then, he passed the days in constant dread of the future, and of himself.

That long silence on the bank of the river continued the rest of the day. About evening, the sleeper wakened. He remained restless from that point until midnight. Torridon managed to give him a little more broth, but, after eating, Black Beaver became more restless still. His fever seemed higher. Throughout the night he groaned continually, and sometimes he broke out into frightful peals of laughter.

After midnight it was plain that he was weakening. The squaws, with desperate, drawn faces, sat by the bed, and their eyes wandered continually from their lord and master to the face of Torridon. He felt the burden of their trust, but he knew nothing that he could do.

Some hours after midnight, there was a convulsive movement of the sick man. Torridon ran to look at him and found that Black Beaver had twisted over and lay face downward. He did not stir. This time Torridon made sure that death was there.

He touched the back of Black Beaver. To his astonishment, it was drenched with perspiration. He leaned lower, and he could hear the deep faint breathing of the Cheyenne.

Once more the power had been granted to Torridon. One more life was saved. He looked up reverently to the black of the trees, to the fainter blue-black of the sky beyond, dappled with great stars.

"He will live," said Torridon. And then he added, with irresistible charlatanry: "The underwater spirits have heard me calling to them. They have come and taken the evil spirit away."

VI

When Torridon and Rushing Wind had left the lodge, Standing Bull showed no inclination to depart from it. As a matter of fact, it was rather a breach of etiquette for him to remain there after the man of the lodge had departed—particularly since the squaw, Young Willow, was gone out, also. Nancy Brett was perfectly aware of this; however, she made light of the matter and began to talk cheerfully, in her broken Cheyenne, about the illness of Black Beaver.

The war chief listened to this talk without comment, fixing a grave eye upon her.

However, he finally said, as though to end the subject: "White Thunder will cure Black Beaver."

"He is very ill," said the girl.

"White Thunder," the chief said, "has power from the Sky People . . . over such *matters as this.*" He added the last words with a certain significance.

And Nancy Brett, canting her head like a bird to one side, asked him gravely what he meant.

"Heammawihio," the warrior explained, "is jealous of men on earth. He does not give double power to one man. The great warriors are not the great medicine men."

"White Thunder," said the girl readily, "has led the Cheyennes against the Sioux and beaten them badly. Is not that true?"

"He was with the war party," said the chief in answer. "He saw signals from the Sky People, which they had sent down because they love the Cheyennes. All that he needed to do was to read those signs. He has power to read them. Just as certain of the old men are able to read the pictures that are painted on a lodge. That is all. The eye of White Thunder is clear to read dreams. He has read my *own* dreams."

The girl suppressed a smile. She had listened to many absurd interpretations that her lover had put upon the dreams of the Indians.

However, now she maintained a straight face. Apparently there was more to come, and it was not long before the chief spoke.

"But as for battle," said Standing Bull, "he never is great. He never has counted a coup. In the fight against the Dakotas, he was not in the front rank. He ran weakly behind the others."

"He killed two men. I thought," said Nancy Brett.

"The Dakotas," explained the Cheyenne, "were herded together like buffalo that do not know which way to run. A child could not have missed them with a headless arrow. But White Thunder did not count a single coup. He did not take a single scalp. When the warriors returned home, White Thunder was not seen at the war dance. He did not come to the feasts to boast."

"He never talks about what he has done," the girl said readily.

"Of course, he does not," answered Standing Bull. "And the reason is that he knows he does nothing of himself."

"Who has made rain for the Cheyennes and saved them when their corn was dying?" she asked.

"Heammawihio," Standing Bull answered with perfect satisfaction in his face.

The girl was silent, wondering at these speeches. Standing Bull appeared in the camp as the greatest friend to Torridon. Certainly, however, he was attacking him now.

"Then," she said at last, "everything that White Thunder has seemed to do really was done by Heammawihio?"

"Everything," said the warrior. "And since he has done nothing in battle, is it not plain that Heammawihio does not wish to strike through his hand at the enemy of the Cheyennes?"

There was a certain childishness in this species of reasoning that she saw could not be answered. Therefore, she was silent. Another thought was entering her mind. She fairly held her breath.

"In war he is weak," went on the chief. "And that is a sad thing. We have spent many days together. I have waited to see White Thunder strike down a single enemy, or count a single coup, or take a single scalp. He never will do that. His spirit turns to water. I have seen his knees shake and his face turn pale." His lip curled as he spoke.

"I don't think that you understand him," she ventured at last. "He always has been very high-strung and nervous. He's not like other men. But I've seen him ride a wild horse that even Roger Lincoln could not ride. And I've seen him stand up to a bully three times his size. He may tremble and turn pale, but he's not afraid to attempt all sorts of things."

Standing Bull merely shook his head. "You," he said, "are a woman, and you know nothing about battle. But I know about battle. I understand such things. You should believe what I tell you."

To this blunt speech, no rejoinder was possible.

"You, just now," went on the chief, "think that he is a very great man. You look on him kindly. You love White Thunder. Is that true?"

She answered frankly: "That is true."

"Women," said the warrior after a moment of gloomy reflection, "are like children. They see the thing that is not and they believe it to be true."

"Perhaps," she said, rather afraid to contradict him.

"Yes, it is true. All wise men know that this is true. So you look like a child at White Thunder. You see that the children follow him, expecting marvels, and the young men talk about him, and the old men ask for his voice in the council. You would say, therefore, that the Cheyennes have no chief greater than White Thunder."

"I would say that he is a great man among the Cheyennes," she agreed cautiously.

"But you do not know," Standing Bull went on, "that in their hearts, when they speak among themselves, all the Cheyennes despise this man."

She was struck dumb.

"All," he continued, "except some of the young braves, like Rushing Wind. They, also, do not think clearly. Their minds are full of clouds. But the warriors who have counted many coups and taken many scalps see the truth about this white man."

She listened, seeing that a crisis was rapidly approaching in the conversation.

"After a while," he continued, "even the younger warriors will understand White Thunder. They, also, will smite to themselves when they see him pass. And then how will you feel?"

"If I love him, I shall not care," she answered.

"Why do women love men?" asked the chief. He did not wait for an answer, but he continued swiftly: "Because a man is brave, because he does not fear the enemy, because he breaks the ranks of the Dakotas in the charge and counts coups upon them and takes their scalps."

She could not speak. He was growing more and more excited.

"You think," he went on, "that someday White Thunder will grow older and bolder and that then he will begin to do these things, but you are wrong, for he never will do them. I, Standing Bull, will tell you that, because it is true, and I want you to know the truth." His breast was beginning to heave and his eyes to shine. Then he said: "But there are others among the Cheyennes who have done these things. I, Standing Bull, have done these things. It was I who went out and dreamed by the bank of the river, with the underwater people reaching out their hands for me. It was I who went up among the Sky People and found White Thunder and brought him down to my people. All this is known to the Cheyennes. All the chiefs and even the children know of these things that I have done."

"I have heard them say so," the girl said, still careful to a degree.

"And also in their councils the old men send for me. They put me in a good place in the lodge. The medicine of Standing Bull is good, they say. It is very strong. When I speak, they listen. I have a strong brain. It thinks straight as a horse runs. When I speak, the Cheyennes all listen. Before long, when High Wolf dies, I shall be the greatest of the chiefs. I tell you this, because it is a thing that you ought to know."

"I have heard all the people speak well of you," she replied. "White Thunder praises you, too. He is a great friend of yours."

She hoped that this remark might soften the humor of the chief, but it had a contrary effect.

"He cannot help but be a friend of mine," said Standing Bull. "The Sky People sent him to me. Therefore, he is forced to be my friend, but all the time he hates me in his heart. He knows that I first brought him here. When he ran away, I went after him. I found him among the white men. They had many guns. They were great warriors. They were his friends and they were ready to strike a blow for him. But Standing Bull was not afraid. He went in among them. He took White Thunder as a mother takes a child. He carried White Thunder across the wide prairie and back to the Cheyennes, and all the people shouted and were glad to have the great medicine man among them once more. So White Thunder still pretends to be my friend, but it is only because he knows that I am strong. I am stronger than he is. In spite of all his medicine, I can do what I want with him. He was given to me by the Sky People."

In his emotion and his pride, he swayed a little from side to side, and his voice reverberated through the lodge like thunder.

The girl watched, cowering a little. She felt that there was a touch of madness in this frantic warrior.

"Also," said the chief, continuing rapidly, "I tell you that Standing Bull has counted many coups. When the coup stick is passed and they ask who has counted twelve coups, the other braves sit silent, until I am called upon. I have taken six scalps. With them I am going to make a rich scalp shirt. Those scalps now are drying and curing in my lodge and they make the heart of Standing Bull great.

"Now I tell you why I am saying these things. If you stay with White Thunder, soon you will be ashamed. You will wish that you had married even the poorest of the warriors. You will wish that your man was brave and strong in battle. But I, Standing Bull, offer to take you. I will put you on a fine horse. I will carry you away. We will forget White Thunder. I have spoken."

VII

No speech was possible to poor Nancy Brett. If an indignant denial and upbraiding burst almost to her lips, she forced it back.

This was treason of one man to his friend. But, moreover, it was something else. It was what Standing Bull considered a statement of plain fact. He wanted to spare her a dreadful humiliation and the complete ruin of her life.

He would leave his place in the nation, and for her sake strive to work out a new destiny in another tribe of the Cheyennes. Leaving his lodge, his horses, his wives, his son and daughters, he would begin a new life.

She felt the force of all these things. She felt, too, that if he were repulsed he would become an active and open enemy, not only of her but of Paul Torridon. And what an enemy he could be she was well able to guess.

So, half stunned as all these thoughts swept into her mind, she was unable to speak, but stared first at the chief, and then at the ground.

He took the burden of an immediate decision from her. He rose and said gently: "Men are like midday, clear, strong, and sudden. Women are like the evening. They are full of a soft half light. Therefore, let my words come slowly home to your mind. Then as time goes on, you will see that they are true. I, Standing Bull, shall wait for you."

With this, he wrapped himself in his robe and passed out from the lodge, clothed in his pride, his self-assurance, his vast dignity. She watched him going like the passing of a dreadful storm, with yet a fiercer hurricane blowing up from the horizon's verge.

She wanted to talk to Torridon at once and give him warning of what had happened. But there was no one with whom she could talk except Young Willow.

That bent crone returned to the teepee, carrying wood. When she saw Nancy Brett alone, she cried out in anger, and, casting down her own burden, bade her run to help in carrying in the next load.

Nancy went willingly enough. Any exertion that would take her mind away from her own dark troubles was welcome to her. The squaw, at the verge of the village, where the brush grew, had cut up a quantity of wood, and she stacked the arms of Nancy with a load under which she barely managed to stagger to the entrance of the lodge. Then she pitched it onto the floor and clung to a side pole, gasping for breath. Young Willow, in spite of her years, threw down a weight twice that which Nancy had been able to manage, and, scarcely breathing hard, turned to the girl with more curiosity than unkindness.

"They have let you grow up lying in bed," said Young Willow. She took the arm of the girl in her iron-hard thumb and forefinger.

"Tush," said the squaw. "There is nothing here. There is nothing here." She tossed the arm from her, but then she told Nancy to sit down and rest. On the contrary, the white girl followed her, though Young Willow scolded her all the while they went back to the brush, saying: "What! White Thunder will take your hand and find splinters in it. 'Who has made this child work?' he will say, and he will look on me with a terrible brow."

It seemed to Nancy an ample opportunity to draw from the squaw confirmation of the viewpoint of the Indians concerning Torridon.

She said simply: "I don't think you would be very afraid of White Thunder, no matter what he said."

"You think not?" Young Willow asked shortly.

"Of course not. You are only afraid of men like your chief, High Wolf."

"Why only of him?" asked the squaw, more abrupt than ever.

"He has counted how many coups, and taken how many scalps?" asked Nancy.

"And should that make us afraid?"

"Yes. Doesn't it?"

"Of course it does. High Wolf is a famous warrior. But he never has pulled the rain down out of the sky."

"And White Thunder never has taken a scalp."

The squaw stopped and peered beneath furrowed brows at the girl.

"You are like all the others," she said. "A woman is never happy until her husband beats her. I never could be sure that High Wolf was a great chief until the day when he threw a knife at me. It missed my eye by the thickness of a hair. After that I knew that I had found a master. I stopped thinking about other men. You are the same way. White Thunder is not great enough for you."

It eased the heart of Nancy to hear this talk. Nevertheless, she wanted much more confirmation, and she went on: "White Thunder is very gentle and kind . . . his voice never is harsh . . . of course I love him. But there are other things."

"Like crushing the Dakotas? Like making the rain come down when he calls for it? Like using the birds of the sky to carry his messages and be his spies? Is that what you mean? What other men can do those things so well as White Thunder?"

"He never has taken a scalp," Nancy repeated, recurring to the words of Standing Bull.

"Why should he take scalps?" said the old woman fiercely. "Does he need to take scalps? When a chief has killed a buffalo, does he cut off its tail? When a chief has killed a grizzly bear, does he cut off its claws and wear them as ornaments? No, he lets the other men, the younger men, the less famous warriors, cut off the claws. He gives the claws away. That is the way with White Thunder."

"He never has joined the scalp dance. He never has joined in the war dance and boasted of what he has done."

"The crow can caw and the blackbird can whistle," said the squaw, "but a great man does not need to talk about himself. No more does White Thunder."

"Never once has he counted coup."

"Listen to me, while I say the thing that is true," the other said. "He struck the Dakotas numb. He sent in the young warriors. All the sighting men rushed on the Dakotas, and the Sioux could not strike to defend themselves. With his power, White Thunder could do this. But why should he want to count coups on men who he knew were helpless? That is not his way. He knows that Heammawihio is watching everything that he does. Therefore, he does not dare to cover himself with feathers and scalps, and he does not even carry a coup stick. It is not necessary. His ways are not the ways of the other Cheyennes, and neither is his skin the same color. But you," she added with heat, "talk like a young fool. You bawl like a buffalo calf whose mother has been killed. There is no sense in what you say. You should sit at home and work very hard and thank Heammawihio for the good husband he has given to you. I, Young Willow, have known many men and seen many young warriors. I have been a wife and still am one. But I never have seen a man so great and also so kind as White Thunder."

This speech utterly amazed Nancy. From what she had heard, she rather thought that Young Willow hated the young master for whom she drudged at the bidding of High Wolf. Certainly they constantly were jangling and wrangling, uttering proverbs aimed at one another, to the huge delight of Torridon, and the apparently constant rage of Young Willow.

But now she saw that the sourness of the old squaw was rather a habit of face than a quality of heart. She smiled to herself, and went on with Young Willow to help carry in the next load of wood.

As they drew nearer to the brush, they saw some boys, stripped for running except for the breechclout thong around the hips, getting ready for a race. When they saw the two women, they rushed headlong upon them, yelling.

"What do they mean?" Young Willow cried, alarmed. "What do they want?"

She raised a billet of wood above her head and threatened them, shouting: "You little fools! I am the squaw of High Wolf, and this is the squaw of White Thunder with me! White Thunder will wither your flesh and steal your eyesight if you displease him!"

In spite of these threats, one of the youngsters darted in, took a heavy blow on the shoulder from the cudgel, and caught both Nancy's hands.

She was cold with fear; his grip had the power of a young tiger's jaws.

He shrilled at her: "You are White Thunder's woman. Some of his medicine must be about you. Give me some little thing! I never have won a race! I am smaller than the others. Give me some little bit of medicine, and I shall carry it back to you afterward. Give something to me, and I shall win the race. They will be blinded by my dust!"

He shouted this. Other boys were pressing about her, clamoring likewise, catching at her eagerly. She almost thought that she would be torn to bits.

At her breast she had a small linen handkerchief. She took it and gave it to the first claimant, the small child who had so desperately wanted help. And off he went, whooping with delight.

The children lined up at a mark. Their race was around a tree some distance off and back to the mark again.

"What can that do for him?" said the girl to Young Willow.

Young Willow laughed. "You will see," she said. "Everything about White Thunder is full of magic. Speaking Cloud had not killed game for a whole moon. I loaned him White Thunder's bow. He killed four buffalo in one day."

Nancy might have pointed out that this handkerchief was hers and had nothing to do with White Thunder, but she said nothing. So often it was impossible to speak sense to these people.

In the meantime, the race began. They were off in a whirl, rounded the tree, and came speeding back for the goal.

"Now look! Now! Do you doubt?" Young Willow asked in exultation.

Behold, the bearer of the white handkerchief was sweeping up from behind his other and larger companions. A starved-looking, wizened boy was he, half blighted in infancy by some illness. But now he came like the wind.

The boys in the lead jerked their heads over their shoulders. Their legs seemed to turn to lead. Their mouths opened. They staggered. And the youngster sped past them, half a stride the first to the line.

"White Thunder! You see what he can do?" cried Young Willow.

And even Nancy was a little staggered.

But, for that matter, she had long been convinced that her lover was the greatest of all men.

VIII

For twenty-four hours after the crisis was passed with Black Beaver, Torridon remained close to him, teaching the awe-stricken and joyous squaws how to cook broths for the patient and gradually to increase the food as the strength returned to the sick warrior. With care, there no longer was any danger. Black Beaver was an emaciated skeleton of a man, but his eyes were clear, and the joy of restored life burned in it wonderfully bright.

So Torridon, a tired man, went back to the village. On the way, he encountered a youngster bearing to him in his arms a little puppy, dead and cold. He laid the puppy at the feet of Torridon, made an offering of half a dozen beads from a grimy hand, and then stood expectantly.

It had even come to that—they looked to Torridon to raise the dead to life again.

He stared at the poor dead thing with pity and sorrow. "I shall tell you what I can do," said Torridon. "His spirit has left him and will not come back. But I shall send that spirit into the other world. There it will grow big. When you die in your turn, it will be waiting for you. It will know you and come to your feet."

The youngster stared with round eyes of grief, yet he was a little consoled, and particularly when Torridon helped him bury the puppy and said over the grave a few words of gibberish. He went bounding back to the village, and Torridon followed after, a sadder man, indeed.

He could see that his life among the Cheyennes was drawing toward a crisis. They had demanded of him one impossibility after another. By the grace of a strange fortune he had been able to meet their wishes, but that good fortune could not continue much longer, and with his first important failure, he dreaded the reaction. What would the wild warriors do?

Full of that thought he came back to the lodge and found Nancy waiting for him with an anxious eye. Young Willow was at work outside, tanning a deerskin, so that Nancy was free to tell him all that had happened.

He heard the story of Standing Bull and his treacherous proposal with an air of fixed gloom. They sat close together. And Torridon took out the slender, long, double-barreled pistol, and cleaned and loaded it with care, not conscious of what he was doing, though the girl read his mind clearly.

What could she say to him, however? What resource was left to them?

The suggestion that came was out of another mind.

Rushing Wind came that evening and took Torridon apart from the lodge. They were beyond the camp before he would speak. Then he declared all that Roger Lincoln had planned and announced that he was willing to do his share. Torridon, hearing, was half doubtful of the faith of the warrior. But like a desperate man he was of a mind to clutch at straws.

They made their plans with care. Every day, Torridon and Nancy were to make a habit of riding out from the camp with their guard around them rather late in the afternoon. Because, as Rushing Wind pointed out, in case of an actual attempt at escape succeeding, the closer the fugitives were to the night, the better for them.

The greatest difficulty, beyond that of breaking away from the guards in the first place, would be in finding a proper mount for Nancy. The best they could do was to hope that the finest animal in Torridon's herd would be swift enough for the work. This was a pinto, a strong little fellow, rather short of leg, but celebrated for iron endurance.

Through all this talk, Rushing Wind spoke nervously, uncertainly, as a man who is not at all sure that he is following the course of duty. However, as they turned back toward the camp he finally declared with some emotion: "I have given my word in exchange for my life. And the life of my father has been given to me, also. May I become a coward in battle, White Thunder, and a scorn and a shame to my people, if I do not work for you in all this as if my soul were in your hands."

With that avowal, Torridon had to rest content, though he was well aware of the shifting mind of an Indian, and the changes that a single day might produce in Rushing Wind and in his resolve.

They had no sooner got back to the camp than two eager messengers pounced on Torridon and dragged him off on an errand of the greatest haste.

They carried him to the lodge of Singing Arrow, an old and important member of the tribe. He had passed the flower of his prime as an active fighter, but he was still of great value and much respected in the council. When Torridon entered, he found Singing Arrow sitting, cross-legged, at the side of a young and pretty girl who he had recently taken as a wife. On the other side of the lodge lay a Negro with a close-cropped, woolly head.

And at a single glance he could tell that the Negro and the girl were suffering from one ailment. Their faces were puffed. Their eyes were distended. Their breath was an alarming rattle in their throats.

The story was quickly told. The evening before, Torridon knew that a Negro, apparently a runaway slave, had come to the camp riding a horse that staggered with exhaustion. The Negro himself appeared weak with the long journey from the settlements. And Singing Arrow, out of the largeness of his heart, had taken him into his teepee. Apparently the poor black man was suffering from some highly infectious disease, and it was making terrible progress with the young squaw.

Torridon examined them in wonder. He never had seen such sickness before. The limbs seemed to be shrunken. The bodies and the faces were swollen. On the right arm of the Negro, high up on the inside, there was a hard swelling beneath the skin. On the left arm of the girl there was a similar swelling. They had high fevers. Their eyes were bloodshot and rolled in delirium. Never before had Torridon seen such a thing.

He gave strong advice at once—that the Negro and the squaw be moved to the edge of the camp, away from all the other lodges. That no one from this teepee should so much as speak to other members of the tribe. That the patients should be watched day and night and given only that light broth that was Torridon's staple diet for all the sick of the Cheyennes.

"The evil spirit in the body of the Negro," he explained gravely, "has called on its fellows. They have passed into the body of the squaw. From her, in turn, they may pass into others."

After that he went back to his own lodge, took off the clothes he was wearing, and had Young Willow hang them outside the lodge, with orders that they should not be touched again until a fortnight of wind and sun had passed over them. Then he went to sleep, very troubled. It seemed as though the great disaster that he had been fearing was already upon the Cheyennes.

In the morning, he learned that the Negro and the squaw were in the same condition. The lodge had been moved, obediently, to the verge of the camp, but in doing so neighbors had given help. Torridon shuddered when he learned this story.

However, there was another thing to occupy both Torridon and Nancy. He told her the plan that morning, and, in the late afternoon, they went out together, with Ashur and the pinto. The great chief, Rising Hawk, was in person at the head of their escort on this day. With him were two young braves, scarcely past boyhood, but for that reason all the lighter, on horseback, all the wilder and swifter as riders.

They passed far down the bank of the river, turned, and rode in a broad circle back toward the village.

As they came nearer, a frantic horseman approached them. His news he shouted from a distance, and again in stammering haste as he came closer. Every person in the lodge of Singing Arrow was prostrate and helpless with the illness. The Negro who brought the pestilence into the village was dead. And half a dozen of those who had helped in the removal of the lodge that day were already ill.

What was to be done? Already the medicine men of the tribe were hard at work, purifying the lodges, treating the sufferers, but so far they had not driven away a single devil from one sick man's body.

Riding hastily back toward the town, they passed the sweat house in time to see a naked man issue from it and run with staggering steps down to the river, accompanied by a medicine man who, with the head of a wolf above his own and a wolf's tail flaunting at his back, bounded and pranced at the side of the sick man.

"Stop them!" cried White Thunder. "That will kill the poor man!"

"Who can stop a doctor when he is in the middle of a rite?" asked Rising Hawk in sharp reproof. "If your own medicine is stronger, go heal the rest of the sick, White Thunder!"

A harsh voice had Rising Hawk as he uttered this dictum, and Torridon made no reply. He merely glanced at Nancy, and she back to him.

He went back to his lodge, took off his clothes, and donned the suit that he had worn on the evening before when he entered the lodge of Singing Arrow, and began a round of the teepees that had the sick in them. Every case was exactly the same, except for one girl who seemed to be in great pain. The others suffered no agony—only a numbing fever that made them unwilling to move, even to eat.

In every case he made the same suggestion—that the whole lodge be moved away from the camp, and a city of the sick segregated, having no communion with the rest of the camp.

His advice was received with open anger.

"You," said one strong warrior whose son was stricken, "have power in such matters as these. Heammawihio gave you that power and sent you down here to take care of the Cheyennes. Now, why don't you do something to help us? You are only giving us words. You are not doing anything or making any medicine to drive away the evil spirits!"

Torridon went back to his lodge sick at heart. He had the feeling that even a skillful doctor would have had his hands more than full in such a case as this, and he was sure that calamity was soon to fall upon him.

IX

When he had changed from the polluted clothing and washed his body clean, he dressed, and went to the entrance of his lodge. Young Willow came to hold back the flap that he might enter.

"Don't come near me," he told her. "If you so much as touch me, you may die of it. I have been near evil spirits."

"You have washed yourself clean," said the squaw.

"It may be even in my breath," Torridon said bitterly.

"Come," said Young Willow stoutly. "I am not afraid. I have never been a man to take scalps, but I never have been afraid to do my duty. Come in. I have some fresh venison stewing in the pot. You may smell it now. Rushing Wind gave us that for a present."

Nancy came in haste, calling softly to him, but he warned her back sharply.

He sat outside the lodge, and ate some meat from a bowl that was placed at his direction near the entrance. A robe was also passed to him. Wrapped in that, he sat back against the wall of the teepee. Nancy crouched anxiously inside.

It was the quiet of evening. The hunters all had returned. Man and boy and dog had eaten and now rested. Later on, the yearning young lovers would wander out with their musical instruments and make strange noises and singing to their loved ones. But now they were quiet, and the dogs that would begin snarling and howling were now hushed, also.

Dun-colored or gleaming white, like pyramids of snow, the teepees stood shadowy or bright around him. From the open entrances, soft voices spoke. Firelight wavered out upon the night through the mouths of the lodges, or in red needles darting through small punctures in the cowhides. The morrow night would not be like this, Torridon could well guess. There would be wailings and weepings for the dead.

He looked above him. The stars were out, unblemished and clear. He felt a strange connection with them, so much had the wild tales of the Cheyennes about him entered his mind, and a sense of doom came over Torridon.

"Nancy," he said.

"Yes," she murmured. "Are you going to stay there the whole night?"

"I don't dare to breathe the same air that you may breathe after me."

"Paul, Paul," cried the girl softly, "if anything happens to you, do you think that I want to live on after you? And in such a place?"

"I've thought it out," he said. "As long as I'm here, they don't care for your comings and goings. You can do what you please. And this is what you must do. Will you listen?"

"Yes."

"Will you do what I tell you to do?"

"I'll try my best."

"Go out and take the pinto horse. He's tethered behind the lodge. Young Willow has gone to High Wolf. You're free to load the pinto with food and robes and never be suspected. Then lead him out of the village and down toward the river. Mount him and ride across. Keep on steadily to the north. Ride due north and never stop. Keep your horse jogging or walking. You'll cover more miles that way without killing your pony. When the morning comes you'll find Roger Lincoln. He's waiting there to the north for us."

"He's waiting for you, Paul. Not for us."

"You've given your promise to do what I tell you."

"Do you think I could go?" she asked.

"You must. There's no escape for the two of us. I see that now. But there is an escape for you. Find Roger Lincoln, and tell him to go back to the fort. Once you're away . . . I'll find some means of escaping . . . after the sickness is ended and gone."

"But you'll never escape," Nancy sobbed. "You'll be visiting the lodges of the sick and you'll be sure to catch it. Then who will take care of you?"

"Such things are chance," said Torridon calmly. "A man has to face some dangers. This isn't a great one. I don't touch these poor invalids. I don't come near their breath."

"Ah, but I know their lodges will be reeking. Six sick people, perhaps, in one teepee."

"Nancy, we're talking about you. Will you go?"

She answered him with an equal calm: "Do you think that I love you as other women love? I mean, women who can live apart from their husbands? I'm not that way. I'd never leave you unless I were dragged away."

After that, he was silent for a time, trying to find some argument to persuade her.

"You can do nothing for me here," he said. "And you have a father and a mother to return to."

She answered bitterly: "I have no father and no mother. They drove me away from you. Following me, you came to the Cheyennes. Except for my father and mother, we would not be here now, Paul. We would be happy in a home of our own."

"If they did wrong," said Torridon, looking as he spoke into the very heart of things, "they did it for your sake. You must not blame them too much. Besides, our lives have some meaning. Is it right to throw them away?"

Nancy strove to answer; the words were lost and stilled in faint sobs, and Torridon knew that it was useless to talk to her any longer on this subject. She would not leave him. And for the first time in his young life true humility flowed into the heart of the boy, and he wondered at her goodness, and the pure, strong soul of Nancy. He wondered if it had not been planned that all this should happen so that he should find the truth about life and about himself.

A haze drew gradually over the eyes of Torridon. The stars floated in a dim mist of thin, golden sparks. He slept.

When he wakened, the cold dew was in his hair and on his face. And from the distance, at the verge of the Cheyenne camp, he heard strange, high-pitched cries. For a moment they were a blended part and portion of his dream, then, wakening fully, he knew them for what they were—the dirges of lament.

And he could see with the mind's eye the poor squaws disfiguring themselves for warrior husbands, or helpless child, now dead and still.

He prepared himself for the grimmest and saddest day of his life, but all his mental preparations were less than the reality.

Like a dreadful fire the pestilence was sweeping through the Cheyenne camp. In the morning, a warrior and two children lay dead, and thirty more were sick. But by noon the sick numbered more than fifty, and they were scattered through all parts of the camp.

The medicine men, frantically rushing here and there, were working in a frenzy to cast out the wicked spirits. But they themselves soon paid for their rashness. Four of them were stretched helplessly by noon in the heat of the day, two of them howling with appeals to the spirits and with pain.

And Torridon went everywhere, grimly, from lodge to lodge. Men and women looked at him with stony eyes, heard his advice with glares, and in silence let him retire. And it began to appear to Torridon that this calamity was blamed upon him as a thing done to the whole nation out of personal malice.

He could have smiled at such childishness, but behind the sullen silence of those red men there was all the danger of drawn knives and leveled rifles. Before noon came, he knew that death was not far from him, if he had to remain in the camp.

He waited until the sun was sloping into the far west, its heat half gone. Then he mounted Ashur, and Nancy Brett joined him on the pinto.

For that was the day of days, so far as they were concerned. Rushing Wind was in command of the guard upon Torridon. And with him were two young braves.

In silence they rode out of the camp toward the river, but as they did so, young Rushing Wind was saying to the white man bitterly: "Why is it, White Thunder? What have the Cheyennes done to you? Why don't you drive away the bad spirits?"

"Rushing Wind," said Torridon, "I haven't the power to do this thing."

"Ah, my friend," said the young brave, "I saw my father lying dead. You brought him back to life."

"He was not dead. He was only very sick."

"His eyes were half opened. His breath did not come," said Rushing Wind. "To you that may not be death, but, to us, it seems death. But in a short time, you made my father strong. Already he sits up against a buffalo robe and asks for meat. But you, White Thunder, are angry with my people. You wish to punish them. Well, I am your friend and I tell you this as a friend. The Cheyennes are growing desperate. Some warrior who sees his son dying, some squaw who sees her strong husband falling sick, may run at you with a knife."

Torridon made no reply.

For just then, out of the village, rode Rising Hawk, and with him were two tried and proved warriors, and they came straight toward Torridon and Rushing Wind.

Had some whisper of the plot to escape come to the ears of this stern young chieftain?

However, when he joined them he gave Torridon a quiet greeting, and simply fell in with the rest of the escort.

"What does it mean?" Torridon murmured to Rushing Wind.

The latter leaned far over and pretended to fumble at his girths. At the same time he whispered: "Give up any thought of escaping today. Rising Hawk suspects something, and he has come here to watch."

Torridon straightened in the saddle and drew a great breath. He had no doubt that Rushing Wind spoke the truth, but he also felt a vast assurance that unless he managed to escape on this day, he never would live to leave the Cheyennes on the morrow. Even as they rode down toward the river, the wailing from the camp followed them from afar, like the screaming of birds of prey in the distance.

X

Rising Hawk was not the only addition to the guard. Presently Standing Bull was seen coming out from the village, armed to the teeth and riding on a dun-colored pony, celebrated as the fastest of his string.

Unquestionably it looked as though the Cheyennes had heard some whisper of the proposed plan to escape. Nancy Brett swung her pony a little closer to Torridon.

"You look like death," she said. "You must smile . . . talk . . . do something to keep them busy and get their eyes off you. Start a game."

"What game could I start?" Torridon asked heavily, for hope had left him.

"Horse racing, then?"

"Against Ashur? They know that they wouldn't have a chance."

"Give them a flying start. Paul, Paul, this is our last chance. Do something."

Her energy and courage shamed him into making some sort of attempt.

He said cheerfully to Rising Hawk, as that dignitary came up: "Here are the fastest ponies among all the Cheyennes. Which is the finest of them all, Rising Hawk?"

The latter swept his glance over the number. "Who can tell which horse will win or which one will fail?" said the chief.

"Ah, well," Torridon answered, "Standing Bull would have made a longer answer than that. He knows that his dun horse is the best one in the tribe."

Rising Hawk turned, and the long eagle feathers stirred behind his head. "It is wrong," he declared sententiously, "to count a coup before the enemy has been touched. And no scalp is taken until it hangs at the saddle bow. There is the horse of White Thunder himself. Does he compare his pony with yours?"

"My horse," Torridon said, as though carelessly, "came from the sky as everyone knows. Standing Bull was comparing his horse with the others that were raised on the prairie. For my part, I think that your own pony, Rising Hawk, would throw dust in the eyes of the others. I have a good hatchet, here, that I would be willing to bet, if you were to run as far as to those trees and back."

It was, in fact, an excellent hatchet of the best steel, and the handle had been roughened and ornamented by the sinking of many glass beads into the wood. When Torridon picked out the hatchet from the sling that held it, Rising Hawk watched with glittering eyes.

"*Hai!* Standing Bull!" he called. All the warriors drew near. "White Thunder thinks that my pony is the fastest of all these. He offers to bet his hatchet."

Standing Bull expelled a breath with a sort of groan. "You have a good horse," he said, "and the horse has a good rider. But I would ride for the sake of that same hatchet."

There was not a warrior in the band but had the same thought.

A course was suggested to a tree half a mile away and back. Suddenly there was dismounting and looking to girths. But Rising Hawk said sullenly: "The rest of you ride. I shall stay here with my friend, White Thunder."

The first hope of Torridon disappeared like a thin mist. Rising Hawk did not intend that the prisoner should escape so easily. He would make surety doubly sure.

However, Torridon added in haste: "I'll ride in the same race with you. Why not? I shall start fifty steps to the rear of the others. Perhaps I can catch you."

"Perhaps," Rising Hawk said with a satisfied smile.

And, in an instant, they had lined up their horses.

Nancy Brett was to have her part, which consisted in holding her own pony to the side of the others and dropping her raised arm as a signal. Torridon reined back black Ashur to the rear. He gave Nancy one fixed look as he did so, and she nodded ever so slightly in return.

They understood one another. The heart of Torridon turned to ice, and all his nerves quivered like wires under a breaking strain. In the meantime, the Cheyennes had gathered at the mark. Every moment, Torridon expected Rising Hawk to call him closer. But though that chief twice turned in his saddle and marked the distance to which Torridon had withdrawn with the black horse, still he made no objection.

The attention of every Indian was now occupied with his pony. Those keen little animals, as though they knew what was wanted of them, began to rear and pitch and kick, and when they lined up, first one and then another strove to dart away.

Several heart-breaking minutes passed in this fashion. But at last the hand of Nancy fell, and the Cheyennes were off the mark with a loud grunting of the ponies as they struggled to get at once into full stride.

Nancy followed then one instant with her eyes. Then Ashur bore down on her.

As keen as any of the Indian horses for the race, the great black stallion had started with a lurch that almost tore Torridon from the saddle, but in an instant he had mastered the big horse with a touch on the reins and a word. He swerved to the left, and, turning her agile little pony around, Nancy fell in at the side of Ashur.

They made straight for the river, above the rocks, where the bed fanned out very broad, and a horse could be ridden easily and quickly through the shallows.

At the top of the bank, they looked back and saw that the furious riders were still rushing ahead for the tree that was the turning point of their race. Rising Hawk, true to his promise, was beginning to forge into the lead.

When they turned that tree, they would see that Torridon was not with them—was not in sight. And they would come like demons to catch him again.

This was the heart-breaking moment of the escape for the two. They gave each other one pale-faced glance, and then their horses dipped down the bank. They struck the water with a splashing of spray. Still, the blinding mist dashed up against their faces as the animals struggled through the shallow current.

At last, firm ground was under the hoofs of their horses. They could see again, and above them, dancing on the top of the bank, they saw an Indian boy of thirteen years or more, with a bow in his hand—dancing from side to side, his arms outspread to stop them, and his voice raised to an anxious scream as he called for help.

Help was coming up to him rapidly, moreover. The boys from the swimming pool, flashing ashore and catching up bows, stones, little javelins, went leaping up the bank and then racing for the danger point.

Torridon knew those youngsters well enough and dreaded them. They had no war bows, to be sure, but they were accurate to a wonderful degree with their play weapons. And a well-placed shaft might kill. Those stones and javelins, too, would make a formidable shower.

But now Ashur and the pinto were struggling up the bank.

They gained the ridge. Torridon pointed his double-barreled pistol at the young Cheyenne, and he turned and bolted with a yell of terror, dodging from side to side to avoid the expected bullet.

Backward glanced Torridon, and he saw the seven racers coming in a wide-flung line, and their shouting went before them, cutting the air with a sound more dreadful than the whistling of whips.

Those shouts had sent the alarm into the village. Other men and boys were darting out from the teepees. Still others were seen rushing to catch horses.

And the heart of Torridon sank in him. For Ashur he had no fear. But how could Nancy on her pinto outride these savage horsemen?

The cloud of youths came like a torrent at them. An arrow hissed past Torridon as he gave Ashur his head, and away they went across the plain, north, due north, where Roger Lincoln, in the dim distance, must be waiting for them according to his promise.

Heaven bring him close—Roger Lincoln and the magic of his long rifle.

The air was filled with the glancing points of javelins. Stones leaped still farther forward into the valley. Arrows arched bravely after them. But neither the pinto nor Ashur was so much as touched. Their speed was great, and the boys were overanxious and at too long a distance.

But that was a small consolation.

At the very first bound, the black stallion had drawn away from the little pinto and had to be pulled back. Running infinitely within his mighty strength, still he was able to keep the pony extended to the uttermost. He seemed to be floating along, and the little pinto was working with all its might.

Nancy, with the same anxious thought in her mind, looked up at Torridon with dread. But she made herself smile, and at that, the heart of Torridon swelled almost to bursting with pride in her courage, with love for her beauty, with pity for the terrible fate which he saw so close before them.

There would be no mercy for him on this second time when he tried to escape. They had spared him before, but now they had watched their best braves sickening, and they had attributed their fall to Torridon's own malice. They would have his scalp and return with Ashur to the village.

As for Nancy? He dared not think of that.

A wild wave of noise broke over the nearer bank of the river. It seemed impossible that the Cheyennes should have crossed the water so quickly, but there they came, every one of the seven racers, still riding abreast in a line that flashed like polished metal in the sun.

Torridon looked back at them almost with exultation in their skill that was redoubling the speed of their horses. He had been among these people so long that, in spite of himself, some pride in their prowess could not be kept out of his mind.

He looked again at Nancy Brett. On her, more than on her horse depended the result of the race, and the first real hope came to Torridon when he saw that her pallor was decreasing, and the color beginning to flare up in her cheeks.

XI

After all, it is not altogether strength that rides a horse, but balance, spirit, rhythm—or otherwise the greatest jockeys would be those of the strongest hands. So Nancy Brett rode well, her heart in her work, her body light in the saddle, and the stout little Indian pony flying over the ground.

They held the rushing Cheyennes behind them. Aye, and then they began to draw away, slowly and surely. So that Torridon, looking to the west and seeing the sun declining with rapidity, laughed aloud in his joy. A trembling laughter, however, so close was his terror on the heels of his exultation.

"We're winning, Nan!" he called to her. "They're falling back! They're falling back!"

She gave him a flashing smile, then returned seriously to her work, putting all her care into it—just a sufficient pull to keep up the pony's head and make it run straight, and always with her eyes before her, if perchance dangerous holes should open in the ground, or to swerve from obvious soft spots.

He, watching her, gloried in her courage and in her spirit. And never had he loved her as he loved her then, when her good riding seemed about to win.

But when he looked back again, he saw that they no longer drew away; the Cheyennes stuck stubbornly at one distance behind them.

Then he remembered with a sinking heart what had been told him more than once before—that good riding on an Indian pony in time of need consists in torturing from the suffering little hardy creatures the last ounce of force. There was an old saying, also, that a horse that a white man had abandoned as useless from exhaustion would still carry a Mexican two days, and when the Mexican gave it up, an Indian could wring another week's travel out of its pitiful bones and stumbling feet. So Torridon kept careful watch behind, never communicating his fear to the girl.

He saw the sweat beginning to run fast from the flanks of the little horse. Then the shoulders were varnished with foam, and foam also flew back from its mouth. If only he could have transferred by magic some of the supreme quality of Ashur to this short-legged running mate. For the lordly Ashur still floated serenely forward, careless, at ease, turning his proud head from side to side, seeming to mock the leagues before him, and the foolish pursuers.

The sun, too, seemed to stick at one place, in the west, refusing to descend lower, so that Torridon could believe the miracle in the Bible. To the slaughtered host, it must surely have seemed that the night would never come, as it seemed now to anxious Torridon.

When he looked back again, he told himself that the distance between them and the Indians was as great as ever, but he knew in his heart that it was not. The pursuers were gaining, little by little.

But it was no time to alarm the girl. She was riding well, closely, with all her attention and skill. Let the Cheyennes press still closer before she began to use the whip.

She would not waste attention, or run the risk of throwing her pony out of its stride by turning to look behind, but from time to time she flashed a glance at Torridon, as though reading the progress of the race in his face.

He knew he was growing pale. He tried to smile at her, and he knew that the smile was a ghastly mockery, because she blanched, and leaned lower over the saddle bows, trying to transfer her weight forward a little and so ease the running muscles of the horse.

At last, glancing back, the leaders of the Cheyennes seemed literally devouring the space left between them and the fugitives. And now into the lead two were racing.

They were well-mounted boys, scarcely established as warriors, but already known for their skill and their daring on the warpath. Light in the saddle, keen as hawks for their cruel work today, they were at their best, and they forged steadily into the lead until, at last, one of them yelled loudly in triumph, and the other, as though spurred on by the shouter, snatched out a heavy pistol and discharged it.

Torridon could not hear the sound of the ball. He felt that they were still too far off to be damaged by such a fire, but he glanced eagerly at Nancy. She gave him that quick, bright smile that meant that all was well.

"The whip, Nan!" he cried to her.

"It's no good," she answered. "He's doing his best."

"The whip! The whip!" he begged.

She obeyed, cutting the little fellow resolutely down the flank, and the result showed that Torridon was right. The little horse, tossing his head, certainly added to his pace.

More and more that hawk-like pair fell to the rear. And ease began to come again over poor Torridon. Still he was by no means sure. Struck by the whip from time to time, the pony certainly was giving his best now. He was strung out straight as a string from head to tail. Foam and sweat ran from him, and his nostrils strained wide, showing the fiery-red lining as he strove to take down deeper breaths of the vital air.

And well and truly was he running, for he was standing off the prolonged challenge of the fastest mounts in that section of the Cheyennes.

Slowly, slowly the sun began to sink. It entered the region of the horizon mist, which stood well up above the level of the plain, and as it turned from fire to gold Torridon smiled faintly and looked again to Nancy. She was looking a bit white and drawn, now, but she never flinched, and well it was that her nerve remained steady and true.

For again the Indians were coming. The main body was some distance back, but the two young falcons in the lead were rushing forward with a wonderful velocity. Torridon could see that with hand and heel they were tormenting the poor horses into greater efforts. There simply was not strength in the arms of Nancy to equal those torments, and, if there had been, she had not the heart for such riding.

So Torridon spoke no more to urge her. He did not need to speak, for every glance she cast at him showed her the agony in his eyes, and that was more than shouted words to her.

Far ahead he saw the streak of shadow that showed where trees were rising above the level of the plain. There, he felt, might be shelter, but he knew in his heart that there was no shelter whatever. It could be no more than the fringing of trees along the bank of a small stream that cut through the plains, and in such a meager wood there would not be a moment's hiding from the sharp eyes of the Indians.

Even that shelter it seemed impossible they should make, for the Cheyennes were pressing closer and closer.

"Nan, Nan," he cried, "for heaven's sake make one grand effort!"

The brave flashing smile she gave him once more and began to jockey the pony as though she were sprinting him over a short course.

He looked back and studied the situation again.

They were neither losing nor gaining, now. Her utmost effort was just able to maintain the pace of the pursuers. Looking back, Torridon could see what had happened to the rest of the Cheyennes.

Well behind the two young leaders was a group of some half a dozen braves, among them Standing Bull and Rising Hawk, and counted among the rest, the finest horsemen among the Cheyennes. But the bulk of the leaders were off on the horizon's verge.

So much the pinto had done, at least. He had sunk the majority of the Cheyenne riders. Only the chosen few remained. But Torridon groaned as he gazed back at them. Two young devils worked in the lead. Behind them came the cream of the entire nation.

The screen of trees before him was all to which he could look forward. After that, death, perhaps. He would not let his mind go past the rising shadow.

Night, at least, would not come down in time. The sun's lower rim was barely touching the horizon, and afterward would be the long twilight—and now every moment was more than hours, sapping the strength that remained to the pinto. Gallantly, gallantly he ran, but he had not on his back a torturing fiend to make of him a super-horse.

Now, glancing forward again, Torridon saw the screen of green rising straight before him. Beyond it was the gleam of water. Was it a fordable place? He hoped so, because the Indians behind did not swerve off to either side.

He said to Nancy: "Ride straight forward. Take the water, but not too fast, and let him walk up the farther bank. Then use what strength is left him to ride him on across the plain."

She stared at him with great eyes. "What do you intend to do, Paul?"

He shouted furiously: "Are you going to argue? Do as I tell you!"

Her head sank a little. He felt as though he had struck her in the face, but he cared nothing for that. He had determined on a last desperate bid for their safety—for a moment's hope in their flight, at the least.

Now he was riding through the thin screen of the willows, and, as he did so, he checked the black stallion and whirled him around; the pinto already was at the water, striking it with an almost metallic crash.

As he whirled the horse about, he saw the two young Cheyennes converge their horses a little, making for the gap between the trees through which the fugitives had ridden, and now Torridon could see the grins of unearthly joy on their faces, the wild glitter of their eyes. Already they were tasting the pleasure of the coup, the death stroke, the scalping.

As for Nancy, she would be reserved—for the teepee of Standing Bull.

He raised his pistol. Both shots must bring down a man, for otherwise it would mean sudden death, clutched by the other young tiger.

They saw that movement. One of them raised his lance and hurled it, but his horse at that moment stumbled, and, although the range was short, the long, slender weapon went past Torridon's head with a soft, wavering hum that he would never forget to his death's day.

The second had caught his rifle to the ready, and from this position he fired it, missed grossly, and then swung the heavy weapon with both hands, making ready to use it as a club to dash out the brains of the white man, and the while riding and guiding the pony with the grip of his powerful knees alone.

For a fraction of a second Torridon had held his fire. Not that there was no fear in him. He was cold with it. But as had happened before in dreadful crises of his life, that fear was not benumbing. It left his brain perfectly clear. He gave the first barrel of the pistol to the left-hand man—the lancer, who had now jerked a war club from his saddlebow. And the long years of practice that Torridon had given to that little weapon were useful now.

He took the head for his target and saw the young warrior slung from his saddle as though struck by a vast weight. The second barrel he gave to the other rider. There was no time, now, for delicate precision in aiming. He shot the man through the body and saw the grin of exultant triumph turn to a ghastly expression of horror, agony, and dreadful determination.

With the long rifle balanced for the blow, the brave rushed his pony in. Just above the head of Torridon the danger swayed, and then glanced harmlessly to the side.

The youth struck the ground with a strange and horrible jouncing sound, like the fall of a half-filled water barrel, and rolled rapidly over and over.

Two riderless ponies turned right and fled, frightened, among the trees.

XII

It affected Torridon, at that moment, like a rush of wind against him. And indeed, the dust that the horses of the two dead men had raised was still blowing up against his face. No, not like the passage of wind, but the light of two dim spirits, suddenly launched into nothingness on this calm, clear, beautiful evening.

For the sun was just down. A pillar of golden fire streaked up the western sky, and, on either side of it, broad wings of crimson, feathered with purple cloud, stretched far north and south, where the horizon was all be-dimmed with soft, rich colors in a band that mounted from the dun-colored earth to the incredible green of the lower sky. And above this, still, there was the evening sky, half glorious with day, and half darkened by night.

But out of that beauty rode a level rank of warriors, each a tower of strength, each terrible, now, to avenge the blood of the dead men. Seven noble Cheyennes, the glory of their race. He knew Standing Bull and Rising Hawk of old. And the others were not a whit less formidable. One of them, tipping his long rifle to his shoulder, sent a bullet hissing past the very ear of Torridon. A snap shot—and yet accurate enough even at that distance almost to end the boy's days.

Then he swerved Ashur away. The stallion crossed the water with a crash and a bound, flung up the farther bank, and went after Nancy Brett and the pinto. When Torridon saw the distance to which she had gained, he was amazed and delighted. He was less pleased when he observed the manner in which Ashur ran up to the pony as though it were standing still.

Nancy, as he came back, turned on him a look as of one who sees the dead returned to life, but she asked no questions. Only when the seven wild riders topped the bank of the river behind them with a yell, she cast one look to the rear.

No doubt she marked the greater distance at which the pursuit rode. No doubt she saw that the two keen hawks of the Cheyennes were nowhere in view. But when she looked forward again, she made no comment to Torridon.

They crossed a little mound in the plain; suddenly the pinto tossed its head. So suddenly did it stop that Ashur was jerked far ahead in his stride before Torridon, his heart still, could swing the stallion around.

He saw Nancy clinging to the neck of the pony, which stood, dead lame, with one forehoof lifted from the ground. Only by grace of good riding and perfect balance had Nancy been able to keep on the horse at all.

Torridon rushed the black to her and held out his arms. "He'll carry us both!"

"It's death for both of us," answered the girl. "Let me go. They . . . they'll pay no attention to me . . . they'll ride on after you." He answered her: "Standing Bull's riding with them!"

Leaning from the saddle, he drew her up to him, and Ashur went off with a swinging stride.

The Cheyennes, speeding behind them, raised a long cry. It seemed to Torridon that that wolf-like howl never would die upon the air. It rang, and floated, and rang again, curdling the blood. Like wolves, indeed, when they make sure of the kill.

And yet the stallion ran with wonderful lightness. It seemed to Torridon, at first, that he marked no difference in the length or the rhythm of the stride. Certainly they were walking away from the red men in the rear.

But a difference there was. Nancy, clinging behind, made a secondary load that could not keep in perfect rhythm with the man in the saddle. It was not sheer poundage, only; it was the clumsy disposition of the weight that would kill Ashur.

But he showed no sign of faltering. He ran on into the red heart of the sunset, when the clouds in the sky took the full color, and almost the evening seemed brighter than the day—blood bright it was to Torridon, and like a superstitious child he caught that thought to his soul of souls and told himself that this was the end.

Back, far back fell the Cheyennes. But then they came again. Torridon, looking back, groaned with despair. It seemed as though magic were in them, to come and come again over those weary miles of long running.

The blood-red moment passed. The sky was old gold and pink and rose and soft purples all about. And still Ashur ran on, with his double burden, against the chosen horses of the Cheyennes.

It had told upon him, however. His ears no longer pricked. And his stride was shortened from its old smooth perfection. The flick and spring were gone from his legs, and in their place came a dreadful pounding that made Torridon bite his lips in sorrow and despair. Yet it was better, was it not, that all three of them—man and horse and woman—should die together?

So said Torridon, in his despair.

And then came a voice at his ear like the flutter of the wind: "Oh, Paul, heaven forgive you if you throw yourself away for me. Your life is more than my life. If you live, my soul will watch you, dear. Paul, Paul, let me go!"

He merely clutched one of the hands that she was trying to withdraw from around him. And he drew the pistol, which he had reloaded as he rode up to her from the river. It was pitifully short in range. They could circle and kill him from a distance. But at least one bullet from it would keep Nancy from them.

The time was not long.

Now, looking over his shoulder, he saw their line extending from side to side as they rushed up on him. They had had their lesson in the killing of the two headlong young warriors, and no practiced brave would throw away a single chance of safety. They saw that their prey was in their grasp, and they were aiming at a circle in which they would net him.

The fastest horses went to either flank, surging gradually forward. The slower remained behind, and one of those was Standing Bull. Torridon felt that he could almost see that face, transformed with greedy passion.

Already the flank horses were drawing up to a level with them, and the braves in the lead, looking inward, regarded Torridon with steady glances.

Though from a distance, though in the dusk of the day, he knew them. He knew their hearts.

He turned still farther in the saddle and kissed the lips of Nancy Brett. "Nan," he murmured, "are you ready?"

"Ready," she said.

"I'm going to stop Ashur and make him lie down. I'll fight from behind him as well as I can. But if they rush me . . . the first shot . . ."

"Yes," she said. And she opened her eyes more widely, and smiled at him without a trace of fear, without a trace of regret, as though to her, dying with him was more than life with any other.

So, in an agony of grief and of love, he looked into her eyes.

A rifle rang. A wild yell burst from behind them, from around them. And then Nancy was crying out in a loud, excited voice.

His own eyes were dim. He had to dash his hand against them before, looking where she pointed, he saw a riderless Indian pony, and the Cheyennes scattering this way and that.

Not fast enough, it seemed, for the gun spoke again, and Torridon saw Young Crow, veteran of many a war raid, peer of all horse thieves, slayer of three Pawnees in one terrible battle, throw up his arms and topple slowly from the saddle, and then roll in a cloud of dust.

The other five, swinging their mounts around, made off as fast as their ponies would bear them from the range of this terrible marksman.

But Torridon, through the thicker shadow that lay along the ground, had marked the flash of the rifle from the top of a rising swale of ground. And he turned to it with an hysteria of joy swelling in him. He tried to speak, but only weak, foolish laughter would bubble from his lips.

Nancy could say the word for him, and her voice was like a prayer of thankfulness: "Roger Lincoln. Roger Lincoln. Thank the heaven that sent him."

XIII

As they swept up to the swale in the golden dusk, they saw Roger Lincoln rise from the grass on his knees and beckon them down to the ground. He wasted not a word on them, but, laying one rifle beside him, he began to load a second with rapid skill, all the while staring keenly through the dim light at the Cheyennes, who had wheeled together and were apparently consulting, though well out of rifle range.

Torridon and Nancy were on the ground before the big man stood up and greeted them. Even then he had barely a word for them, and the thanks that began to pour from the lips of the girl he hushed with a wave of his hand. He went on to the stallion and stood before him, hands clasped behind his back, and brows frowning.

"Here's the weak spot," said Roger Lincoln, "and it's the very spot that I thought would be strong."

He turned with an impatient exclamation and stared at Torridon. One would have thought that he was angry with him, and Torridon said feebly: "We started with Nancy on the best pony we could get, Roger. The pinto went lame, and Ashur has been carrying us both."

"I could see that," Roger Lincoln said tersely. "You," he added sharply to the girl, "get on Comanche. Comanche, stand up!"

Out of the grass rose the famous silver mare, and beside her a tall brown gelding, the very make of speed—lean-headed, long of neck, with shoulders that promised ample power and a deep barrel—sure token of wind and heart.

"Take the brown," said Lincoln to Torridon, "and lead Ashur. We have to cool him out, and it won't do to let him stand."

"And what will you do, Roger?"

"I'll run."

Nancy was about to protest, but Torridon himself silenced her. "Lincoln knows best," he said. "Do as he says."

He helped her into the saddle. Roger Lincoln already was running lightly before them at a stride and pace that seemed to show that he intended a long jaunt. And he bore due north.

As Torridon sprang into the saddle on the gelding, he heard Nancy murmuring: "He's furiously angry, Paul. What have we done?"

"He's not angry, I hope," said the boy. "But he's thinking hard about how he can get us out of this trouble. There's nothing else in his mind. Don't doubt Roger Lincoln. Doubt me, sooner."

He drew on the lead rope, and Ashur broke into a stumbling trot. He was very far spent indeed, with flagging ears and dull eyes. And as Torridon rode, he kept well turned in the saddle and talked continually to the great black.

The last of life seemed to be flickering in the glazing eyes of the stallion, but under the voice of his master that light grew brighter in pulses. The jog trot, also, seemed better for him than merely standing. But still he was very far done, and his hoofs struck the ground, shambling and uncertain, as though they moved by a volition of their own and without the will of the horse. And it seemed to Torridon, as he looked back at the fine head of the horse, that, rather than abandon Ashur, he would stay behind and fight the Cheyennes, single-handed.

The Indians, in the meantime, had spread far and wide across the plain, their five figures gradually dying in the dusk of the day, while Roger Lincoln still ran before Torridon and the girl with a tireless step.

They went on for nearly an hour. The dusk thickened. The last pale glow finished in the west, and then there was darkness, utter and absolute.

Roger Lincoln whirled and stopped the cavalcade. "How is Ashur?" was his first question.

"Tired, tired, Roger. He shambles like a cow."

The scout spent a moment at the side of the stallion and then said briefly: "He's only half a step from a dead horse. Here's a blanket on the ground. Can you make him lie on that?"

The stallion obeyed. Even in the darkness, Torridon could see the knees of Ashur shake violently as his weight came heavily on them.

Lincoln flung another robe over the big black. "Do you know how to rub down a horse, Paul?"

"I know."

"Work on his shoulders and chest. I'll take care of the hind-quarters. You, Nancy, take the head. Rub with a wisp of that grass. We have to keep his circulation going."

He made his own two horses lie down. He had chosen a little depression in the surface of the level prairie. That faint declination of the ground and the height of the grass that grew thickly around it gave them some shelter if the Indians should attempt to spot them against the skyline of the stars. But, at the same time, it allowed the Cheyennes to creep up unobserved in turn. In a way, they had blinded themselves and were now trusting to sheer chance to keep them out of the way of those keen hunters.

But even Nancy knew well enough what this work meant. With two horses they never could escape from those bloodhounds of the plains. With Ashur once again on his feet and capable of his matchless gallop, they had at least a fighting chance.

So all three fell to work in silence, only broken when Roger Lincoln, pausing to allow his aching arms a chance of recuperation, murmured: "When I remember how Ashur pitched me into the middle of the sky . . . and then tried to catch me with his teeth . . ." He laughed softly. And then he added: "But that shaking up was worthwhile. I never would have known you, Paul, except for it."

This was all he said by way of welcoming them. Nancy, from the first, might have been a figure of wood to him, so little atten-tion did he pay to her, but gradually she came to understand. All the heart of that hero of the frontier was bent upon the great task before him. He had no time for amenities. But all the more strongly she began to feel that every drop of blood in his veins was given to the task he had undertaken. He would die most will-ingly to do the thing he had in hand.

"Hush," whispered Roger Lincoln suddenly. It was the ghost of a hiss, rather than a word.

They stopped working. Dimly Torridon saw Lincoln reach for his rifle and gradually bring it into position. He himself drew his pistol. They waited endless moments with thundering hearts. Then something stirred through the grass, and against the stars, not ten yards from them, Torridon saw two riders looming, the faint night light glistening on their balanced rifles. But when he raised his pistol, a hand of iron gripped his arm. He waited. For an eternity, the two Indians sat their horses side-by-side. Torridon could see them turning their heads. They were so near that he could hear the swish of the rising wind through the tails of their horses. And he prayed with all his might that none of the horses might make a sound, a snort, or the least noise of tearing at the grass.

That prayer was granted. Softly as they had come, the pair of ghostly forms moved away again. And at an almost mute signal, the fugitives resumed their work on the stallion.

It seemed to Torridon's trembling touch that the flabby texture of the shoulder muscles had been changing—that the old feeling, like cables of India rubber, was beginning to return to them.

He whispered softly to Roger Lincoln: "I think Ashur could go on now."

"Are you sure?"

"Almost."

"Make sure if you can."

Torridon whispered.

At the mere hiss of sound, the black stallion jerked up his head from the hands of Nancy. "Yes!" Torridon said joyously.

They stood back, and, at Torridon's murmured command, the stallion rose. The other two horses got up, unbidden, and it seemed now to Paul Torridon that they had risen from the warm, secure darkness of the grass to stand among the very stars. Surely someone of those prowling Cheyennes could not fail to see them.

Roger Lincoln was speaking quietly: "The whole crew of Cheyennes are spilled around us over the plain. They may stumble on us in the dark, and, if they do, nothing can keep them from cutting our throats. I think those red men see in the dark, like cats. But, in the meantime, they're spreading their nets for us. I propose to head back straight south, march at a walk for a couple of hours, and then swing toward the west for an hour, then back again toward the north. We may be running our heads into the lion's mouth. If you don't agree to this, we'll try something else. But I think that by this time you'd find more of them to the north than to the south."

It seemed almost rashly bold counsel to Torridon, but he dared not question the wisdom of Roger Lincoln, so often proved—and in times all as perilous as this one. He merely murmured to Nancy: "Have you strength to go on?"

"For days and days," she said. "It's no longer terrible . . . it's a glorious game."

It stunned Torridon to hear her. She, slender as a child and hardly larger, was making of this a game, while his own nerves were chafed to the breaking point.

But he believed her. There was the wavering note of ecstasy in that whisper of hers. And, after all, she came of wild blood, strong blood—the blood of the clan of Brett.

He remembered them now, like so many pictures of giants, striding across his mind, and he told himself that if she lacked their physical size, all the more heart was hers. So she had borne herself among the Cheyennes at the village cheerfully, with a high head, smiling in their faces. And Torridon felt himself growing smaller and smaller in his soul. Roger Lincoln had a right to such a woman as this. But he, Paul Torridon, what claim had he?

They led their horses. Comanche was blanketed lest her silver coat should reach the eye of the enemy, and so they started on that southward march.

XIV

It was an evil time for reflections of any kind. They marched steadily to the south, Lincoln first, Nancy next, and Torridon as the rear guard, his pistol in his hand. Ashur undoubtedly was recovering from the terrible strain of his journey under the double burden. His head was beginning to be held high, and, when they halted once or twice, Torridon felt the flanks and found them firm, no longer drawn by exhaustion. It doubled the courage of Torridon to note these signs.

They marched on for the greater part of an hour, and then a sudden voice cried at them: "Who is that?"

A great, harsh voice in Cheyenne!

Rising from the ground to their right, Torridon saw several Indians, faint against the stars. He himself had no voice, but that of Roger Lincoln made a growling answer: "Standing Bull. Scatter to the west. They are not in the north."

"It is Standing Bull," one of the Indians said in a plainly audible voice.

"How could it be?" said another. "I left Standing Bull only a little while ago, and he was on a fresh horse. Why should he be walking now?"

"Mount," said the soft voice of Roger Lincoln.

And the three of them were instantly in the saddle. The moment Torridon was on the back of the stallion he knew that once more all was well with the great black horse.

"Standing Bull!" called one of the Cheyennes.

Roger Lincoln rode calmly on, still at a walk.

"Look! Look!" cried the Cheyenne who as yet had not spoken. "That is the great horse of White Thunder. There is no other in the world with a neck and head like that!"

Torridon had had a flash of the outline against the stars, and the Indians charged with a yell the next instant. He had a glimpse of Nancy slipping forward on the neck of her horse. He saw the long rifle of Lincoln glimmer at his shoulder, but for his own part he had something better than a rifle to work with. Light in hand, easily aimed, he was as confident of the pistol as though he held two lives in his palm. And a sort of wild ecstasy ran through Torridon. He never had felt it before, but it was as though Indian blood had stolen into his veins, for, swerving the big stallion to the right, he drove him straight at the charging men.

He fired—a tossing head of a horse received the bullet, and down went pony and rider—the Cheyenne with a whoop of rage and dismay. He fired again, and there was an answering half-stifled yell of pain.

There were five in the party. They split to either side before this death-dealing magician.

"White Thunder!" he heard the cry. "The Sky People are fighting at his side!"

And they scattered over the plain.

Torridon found Ashur galloping on, like a set of springs beneath him. Roger Lincoln was ranging on his left side, Nancy on his right. And vaguely he was aware that the great Roger Lincoln had missed his target with the rifle. A long tongue of flame had spurted from the muzzle of the gun, but of the five Cheyennes, only two had fallen.

"Northwest, northwest!" called Lincoln, and swung his horse in that direction.

No doubt the Cheyennes would spread the report that the party was trying to drive south.

Lincoln pulled down from a gallop—a steady jog that would shuffle the miles behind them without exhausting the horses. Plainly he expected more trouble when the morning came, if not before.

But all through that night there was not a sound of a Cheyenne; there was not a sight of them. The gray of the dawn came. They saw one another as black silhouettes. Then features became visible. But first of all they regarded the horses. Ashur, wonderfully recovered, seemed as light as a feather. Comanche was in fine fettle, too, but the gelding that Roger Lincoln rode plainly showed the strain under which it had been traveling. There was now the weak link in the chain.

They came to a thin rivulet. There was only a trickle of water, but they found a fairly deep pool, and there they halted. Much work lay before them before they gained the safety of Fort Kendry.

They washed the legs and bellies of the horses, the men doing the labor while Nancy was sharply commanded by Lincoln to lie down on a blanket that he stretched out for her. Flat on her back he made her lie, her arms stretched wide.

She smiled for a time at the gray sky. A moment later her eyes were closed in sleep.

Torridon, worried, would have wakened her, but Lincoln forbade it.

"If we could make Fort Kendry today," he said, "it would be worthwhile. But we cannot. It's a long march. She has to rest."

"The Cheyennes will never rest on this trail," Torridon assured him. "They'll ride on it like madmen. Roger, they've had six men shot down, and four of them, I think, are dead or nearly dead. Their pride will be boiling."

"They'll never stop," agreed Lincoln, "and they'll never rest as long as they can make their horses stagger on. But we can't go on at this rate, unless we determine to leave Nancy behind us. Help me make a shade over her eyes. Let her sleep as long as she will."

Over two ramrods and a stick they stretched a blanket, and in that shadow Nancy still slept while the sun rose higher and the world was drenched in white, hot light.

The brown gelding and the mare were lying down. Ashur was busily cropping the grass. And the two men, withdrawing to a little knoll from which they could sweep the plain to a distance, admired the stallion.

"Look at him," said Roger Lincoln. "You can't see more than the shadow of his ribs. The work that would have killed two ordinary horses was simply a good little work-out for him. There never will be another like him, Torridon. Never in this world."

Torridon agreed.

Of other things Lincoln talked, half drowsily.

"Four men for you, Paul Torridon. Four Cheyennes, at that!"

"Luck," explained Torridon. "Both times it was a question of quick shooting at close range. That was why the pistol was useful. Might live a long life before such a chance came to me again."

"Only luck?" Roger Lincoln smiled.

"Chiefly," said Torridon. "I don't want you to think that I pose as a hero. I'm not. I've been scared white all through this."

"When you rode down at those five yelling redskins?" Lincoln asked with the same good-humored smile.

"Then," said Torridon, "well, I don't know. Something came over me."

"You yelled as though you were having a jolly time of it," chuckled Lincoln.

Torridon was silent. He could not understand himself, and how could he offer an explanation. But still there was a sort of memory in his throat, where the muscles had strained in that dreadful yell.

He almost felt, in fact, as though another spirit at that moment had entered his body and directed his movements. And there was something disquieting in the calm, curious eye of Lincoln, and the little smile that was on his lips.

"Tell me, Paul."

"Yes . . . if I can."

"You can. This is a simple question, this time. Were you ever so happy as you were that instant, charging the Cheyennes?"

"Happy? Good heavens, of course I've been happier!" exclaimed Torridon.

"Don't be shocked like an old maid, my lad. Think back honestly. Even when Nancy Brett, yonder, told you one day that she'd marry you, were you as happy as when you went through those Indians and split them away before you, like water before the nose of a canoe? Be honest, now."

Torridon, desperately striving for that honesty, suddenly took a great breath. "I think you're right. No . . . I never was happy . . . in the same way, at least. It was a sort of madness, Roger. It really was a sort of wildness in the head."

"But not enough to make your pistol miss."

"They were very close," said Torridon, vaguely feeling that this was not praise, and worried.

"They were riding like fury at you, and you at them. Most men don't shoot straight at a time like that . . . particularly with an old-fashioned pistol." He sat up straight and pointed a finger at Torridon. Every vestige of the smile was gone from his face. "Paul," he said, "you're a grand fighting man, but you never ought to stay on the frontier."

"I don't understand," Torridon murmured. "But, of course, I've no particular desire to stay out here."

"You think not. But . . . don't stay. Go back East and starve, if that's your luck, but don't stay on the frontier."

"Will you tell me why?"

"Because all the men out here are armed to the teeth. And there are plenty of chances for trouble."

"I don't pretend to be a hero," Torridon said a little stiffly, "but I don't think that I'm an absolute coward, either."

"You're not," replied Lincoln, with the same smile, half whimsical and half cold. "You're decidedly not a coward. You're the other thing, in fact."

"What thing, Roger? Unless you mean a bully?"

He laughed at the mere thought. "Not a bully," said Roger Lincoln, "a tiger, Paul. Not a bully."

Torridon stared. "I'm trying to believe my ears," he confessed, "but I find it a pretty hard job."

"Why?"

"Because all my life I've been afraid of people. Terribly afraid of people. They've haunted me. I've lain awake at night, hoping that I'd never meet certain men again."

Lincoln nodded. "You've led the life of a man who fears danger, I suppose," he said dryly. "Think over the skeleton of it. Captured from your own people by the Bretts . . . raised among them and given the sharp side of the elbow all your life . . . made to teach their young bullies in a school, and mastering the roughest of them . . . I know that story."

"I had help . . . I couldn't do a thing with them, with my hands."

"The brain, Paul! The brain is the tool that wins battles of all kinds. After that, you tame a wild horse that no man could handle except you . . ."

"Only by patiently visiting him every day, because I loved him. I never dreamed of mastering him."

"But master him you did. Do you carry him, or does he carry you? When I lay on the ground with more than half a ton of that black stallion charging at me, who stood up and braved him away?"

"Afterward I . . . was sick with fear," Torridon said honestly.

"The girl is sent away. You are thrown into a cellar and kept for a dog's death . . ."

"From which you saved me, Roger, and heaven bless you for it."

"I never could have saved you. We fought our way out, side-by-side. The girl was gone to the Far West. You didn't hesitate to start cruising after her. Was that the act of a timid man?"

"I would have gone anywhere with you, Roger, of course."

"You lost me on the plains. I gave you up for dead, but, just as I gave you up, you turn up at the fort. By heavens, you'd joined the wild Cheyennes, and you'd become their chief medicine man."

"It was a strange combination of circumstances. I did nothing but a few silly tricks for them. Luck was with me tremendously."

"Luck was with Columbus, too," Lincoln said dryly. He went on: "They want you so badly that they follow you on and kidnap you at the fort. When you're not happy among them, they steal Nancy away, too. You take them in the palm of your hand. Finally you break away and carry the girl with you . . ."

"Because you helped me, Roger."

"Don't interrupt. And when they follow too closely, you turn around and kill a pair of their best fighting men."

"They were mere youngsters!"

"Were they? And was that nest of five scorpions that you charged, back yonder, a set of youngsters, too?"

"I had the night to cover me."

"So did they! But you looked through the darkness like a cat and shot down a pair of them."

"I don't think either of them was very badly hurt."

"Paul," said Roger Lincoln, raising his hand gravely, "let me tell you that when I heard that terrible yell come out of your throat, I was frightened. So were those Cheyennes. They ran as if a fiend was after them. And just at that moment, you *were* a fiend. You were in your glory. And I tell you, Torridon, that having had one hot taste of blood, you're going to turn into a man-eater, unless you keep away from temptation . . . such as you'll find on this frontier."

Torridon shook his head with conviction. "I hope I never have to draw a gun again," he said earnestly.

"You think you hope that. You don't know yourself. We're always confusing the self of today with the self of yesterday. We don't understand that we change. Now, you know your history better than I do. But I believe that in the beginning Robespierre hated the sight of blood. Even the blood of a chicken was too much for him. But in the finish, he shed tons of it."

"Am I a Robespierre?" Paul Torridon asked with a faint smile.

"You're not," answered the frontiersman, "but you're the hardest type of gunman and natural killer that steps the face of the earth."

"Good heavens, Roger, what are you saying to me?"

"The gunman who is a bully," said Roger Lincoln, "soon does murder for its own sake, and soon he's disposed of. But the deadly fellow is the quiet man who looks always afraid of the world . . . who always *is* a bit afraid . . . and who loves that fear thrilling in his backbone as a dope fiend loves cocaine . . . the quiet, shrinking little fellow who never speaks without asking pardon, who, nevertheless, by some fatality is always near danger, who always is being forced to draw his weapons. Torridon, if you stay on the frontier six months longer, you'll have killed six men . . . not Indians, Paul . . . white men as good as yourself."

He drew a long breath, and, leaning back on the hummock, he filled his pipe and began to smoke, while Torridon, confused and half frightened, stared at the distance and tried to recognize himself. He could not believe that Roger Lincoln was entirely right, but of one thing he was suddenly sure—that his old self was dead, and that in its place there was a man who he did not know, wearing the name of Paul Torridon!

There was a stir, and Nancy Brett came from beneath her shelter.

"Breakfast time," said Roger Lincoln cheerfully, and got up from the grass.

XV

Whether the Cheyennes had been thrown into confusion by the failure of the fugitives to keep due north in the first place, and their then swinging south, and so had failed to guard the thrust to the northwest, the three were not able to tell at the time. But, going carefully forward, husbanding the strength of their horses as they worked back toward the direction of Fort Kendry, certain it was that no sign of the red men appeared until that wildly happy day when they rode into the fort and there passed in the street, no other than the tall form of Standing Bull, wrapped in a gorgeously painted buffalo robe, his eyes fixed blankly before him, as though he were unable to recognize the party.

Roger Lincoln was for taking the big Indian in hand at once, but Torridon dissuaded him. He pointed out that his relations with Standing Bull had been more friendly than hostile. And, at any rate, they were safely in from their long voyage over the prairie.

They took Nancy to her uncle's house, and Torridon only hung in the background long enough to hear the shrill nasal cry of joy with which her strong-armed aunt welcomed her.

Then, with Roger Lincoln, he went toward the fort.

They were welcomed effusively. On that wild frontier strange exploits took place every day, but there was a peculiar strangeness about the adventures of Torridon and Nancy Brett. The commandant sat them down at his own table, and a crowded table it was to which Roger Lincoln was asked to give the details of the escape. He gave them with the utmost consideration of Torridon, but no matter what he said, the exploits of the boy were passed over. And if some eye lit with wonder and turned on Paul Torridon, the glance turned away again at once. Men want one of heroic appearance to fill the hero's role, and Torridon looked too young, too weak, too timid, in fact, to satisfy. Everyone preferred to cast the entire glory upon Roger Lincoln. He filled the eye. He filled the mind, and he was known to have a long tale of glory in his past. This was treated as a crowning feat.

As for consideration of Paul Torridon, that unlucky youth himself blasted all opportunity when, as the party broke up, he was heard murmuring to his friend: "How shall I ever dare to go to Samuel Brett's house to see Nancy, Roger?"

The remark was repeated with roars of laughter.

Hero? This? Fort Kendry told itself that it knew a man, and it could not be deceived.

But there was more trouble in store for Torridon. Some few lingered with the commandant after the supper party had broken up, and Torridon, with others, had gone to bed. And in the midst of this final chatting, there was a rap at the door, and a huge young man in rather ragged deerskins appeared before them. He wanted Paul Torridon, he said.

"Torridon's not here." said Roger Lincoln. "But I'm his friend. Can I give him a message? He's gone to bed, dead tired. I don't want to disturb him unless it's very important."

The youth in the doorway stepped a little inside and ran his bold eyes over the company.

"It might be important, it might not," he said. "That all depends. My name is Dick Brett. I come out here with my brother Joe. We come hunting for a low skunk and yellow-hearted cur by name of Paul Torridon. We heard he was here. But if he ain't . . . just somebody tell him that I'm gonna be waiting for him in the street in front of Chick Marvin's store tomorrow morning about nine. If he comes and finishes me off, then he can take on Joe. But if he don't come, I'm gonna hunt him down and finish him. I guess that's about all." He waited a moment.

There was an uneasy instant during which the guests half expected Roger Lincoln to attack this slanderer of his friend, but Roger Lincoln said not a word. And Dick Brett departed unhindered.

"What'll be done, Roger?" asked the commandant uneasily. "It's sort of a shame for a kid like that Torridon to be put on by one of Brett's size. Any relation of that same Nancy?"

"Second cousin," Roger Lincoln said smoothly. "And what do you think will happen when Torridon gets this message?"

"He'll be heading back for the open lands," chuckled the commandant.

There was a general nodding of heads.

"And what," said Roger Lincoln, "will happen if he goes out to meet the pair of them?"

"Roger," said one of the trappers, "I like you fine, and I know that you've got brains in your head. But you made a mistake about this here one. He ain't got nothing in him. I looked him in the eye. He dropped his look. He's pretty thin stuff for the making of a man."

Roger Lincoln looked about him with a sigh. "I knew it would come unless I got him away quickly," he said, "but I hoped that I'd have more time than this."

"Before we found him out to be yellow, Roger?" asked the commandant curiously.

"Before," said Lincoln, "you found him out a man-eater. Man, man, do you think I was talking for fun, tonight? Did I tell you he shot four Cheyennes out of their saddles with a pistol during that chase? And I tell you again that he'll never be stopped by those great hulks, the Bretts! Only . . . how can he marry Nancy after he's shed the blood of her kindred?"

"That's sounding talk," said the commandant calmly. "But you know yourself, Roger, that the kid would never dream of coming to the scratch, unless he knew that you'd be there to back him up."

"Then," said Roger Lincoln, "I'll I tell you what I'll do. I'll let one of the rest of you carry the word to Torridon. I'll not go near him tonight or tomorrow. And heaven help the Brett boys, is all that I have to say."

XVI

When Torridon heard the news, he merely lifted his head from the pillow and stared at the commandant with such gleaming eyes that that gentleman withdrew in some haste. He went thoughtfully back to his table companions.

"Roger," he said slowly, "maybe there's something in what you were saying."

But Torridon himself merely lay awake for a few moments, staring into the darkness, then he fell into an untroubled sleep. When he wakened, he found himself singing as he sponged with cold water and then shaved. And in the midst of that singing he paused and struck himself lightly across the forehead with the back of his hand.

It was not as it had been of old. He should be cowering sick at heart in a corner. Instead, there was wine in his blood. And he remembered with a shock what Roger Lincoln had said about the hot taste of blood, never to be forgotten.

He shook that thought away. He had slept late. At 7:30 a.m. he went out from the fort to a vacant field, shrouded with fir trees, all whitened and frosted over by a slowly falling rain mist. He fired ten shots at a small sapling. When it sagged and then toppled over with a sharp, splintering sound, he cleaned his gun thoroughly, reloaded it, and went in for his breakfast.

Breakfast was over. The cook could give him only soggy, cold slices of fried bacon and cold pone, heavy as wood. Yet, with lukewarm coffee, that was a feast to Torridon. The famine of the long ride was still in his bones. He found the cook watching him curiously. When he came out into the big yard of the fort, other men left off their occupations and regarded him with the same wondering, hungry eyes, as though they could not believe what they saw.

He asked for Roger Lincoln. Roger was not there, it appeared. Well, he was glad of that. Roger, at least, would not be there to see the fight. Roger would not be there to accuse him. He felt a sudden pang of shame as he went into the street. Those other men, rifle raised and rifle trained, how could they stand against the subtle speed of a pistol at short range? Ah, well, they were Bretts. What pity need a Torridon show them?

And a terrible joy filled the blood of Torridon. He wanted to laugh and sing. He wanted to run. But he made himself go with a soft, quiet step, with a composed face; what wonder that his eye was fire, then?

He went straight to the house of Samuel Brett. That huge man in person came to the door, and, when he saw Torridon, he roared with rage, and lifted up a hand like a club. From within the house came the sharp call of Samuel's wife, and the shrill cry of Nancy—poor Nancy.

Torridon laid his pistol mouth on the chest of the giant. "I'm going to kill a pair of Bretts," he said quietly, "and then I'm coming back here to find my wife. I expect the door to be open."

He put the pistol away, and turned slowly and walked up the street, and as food to his heart was the memory of the pale, astonished face of Samuel Brett.

He went in the middle of the road, picking his way carefully among the ruts and the puddles. It still rained. Once a gust of strong wind and rain came and unsettled his hat. He paused, deliberately raised his hat and combed the moisture from his long hair with his fingers, settled his locks over his shoulders, replaced the hat, and went on.

There was no one in any house. And, when he arrived there, he found the whole population of the town at the big store. They were like a sea at every door, at every window, and banked across the street—Indians, whites, half-breeds, Negroes, French Canadians, all wild as tigers, but looking to Torridon, suddenly, like a very gentle and rather awe-stricken crowd.

And in the middle of the street stood Dick Brett, huge as a tree and as immovable.

"He has a heart, however," said Torridon coldly to himself, "and even with a pin one could kill him. Accuracy is all one needs."

He walked straight on, while Dick Brett pitched the butt of his rifle into the hollow of his shoulder, aimed—and still Torridon went lightly, steadily toward him. The rifle was lowered. He was close now—pistol close. And yonder at the edge of the crowd, stern of face, was the other brother, rifle ready, too.

"You treacherous, sneaking rat and woman-stealer!" bellowed Dick Brett. "Have you come to fight like a man, or to get down in the mud and crawl?"

"I've come to kill you," said Torridon pleasantly, and drew the pistol. Light, light was the metal in his fingers. He could not miss. It was as though a silken thread drew the muzzle straight to the forehead of big Dick. He, with an exclamation, snatched the rifle butt once more to the hollow of his shoulder. How slow and blundering seemed the motion to Torridon.

There was almost time to pause and smile at it—then he fired, and Brett fell, the gun discharging as he went down, face foremost. And smiling indeed was Torridon as he went on, the pistol hanging at his side. The second brother had disappeared.

There was a whirl and eddy in the crowd where he had been standing, and then red fury took Torridon, and red drunken joy in killing. He ran like a greyhound for a hare. He rushed through the crowd—they gave back suddenly before him, split away as by a vast hand of fear. He hurried into the store. He peered under draped counters and tables. He ran out into the back yard.

Slowly, his teeth gritting, he came back to the street and looked up and down. Another day, then, for the second brother. Then he saw men carrying a prostrate form, a sagging body, toward the door of the store—Dick Brett, who lifted his head a little, despite the red wound in his forehead. That head was turning, and Torridon saw a crimson gash down the side of it. Then he understood—the bullet had slipped off the bone, and glanced around the scalp. He stepped to the wounded man and touched his shoulder.

Fear made the eyes of Dick Brett bulge in his head.

"There will be another day for you and me," said Torridon.

Then he turned back down the street, past white, icy faces, and eyes that looked at him as though he were a column of fire. A great voice called. And there was Roger Lincoln beside him, walking with him toward the house of Samuel Brett.

"Paul," said the frontiersman, "before you go into the house, ask yourself if you're a safe man to be her husband. I warned you about yourself before. Was I right, or was I wrong?"

Torridon paused. And as he paused darkness ran over his brain. He found himself repeating: "What have I done, Roger?"

"Nearly killed one man . . . tried to kill two. And now you're going to marry Nancy Brett to a gunfighter with not three years of slaughter before him, perhaps."

Torridon caught at the arm of Lincoln. "Oh! Oh!" he groaned. "What's happened to me? I don't know myself. Roger, what shall I do? What shall I do? Shall I turn back? Shall I leave Nan?"

Roger Lincoln held him off at arm's length. "You're past the help of any man," he said. "But maybe . . . wait here."

They were in front of the house of Samuel Brett, and Roger Lincoln went into it, leaving Torridon stunned, feeble, in front of the place. The wind was shaking the rain clouds to bits. Long rifts and streaks of blue appeared in the sky. And the poplars around the Brett house began to shine like silver—like silver mist was the smoke that rose languidly from the chimney top.

It was to Torridon like a dissolution of the world, and his own self had dissolved before it. He was a new man; what manner of man he hardly could tell, but those words of Roger Lincoln in the prairie came hauntingly through his mind—he saw the train of his life behind him, the super delicacy, the hypersensitiveness of his body, of his very soul. And brutal chance had taken him in hand and hammered and hardened him until, at last, he had been changed from flesh to metal.

Aye, at that very moment, half his heart was back up the street, yearning to hunt down that other who had fled, savagely yearning.

Something came down slowly toward him. It was a shape of mist to him, in his rush of thoughts. But those thoughts cleared, and like a light through a storm he saw Nancy coming to him. And a wild torrent of emotion made Torridon fall on his knees before her, and take both her hands.

They trembled under his touch.

"Nan," he cried wildly, "tell me, for heaven's sake, that you have no fear of me!"

She drew him up to her, her slender arms about him. "Don't you see, Paul?" she said to him. "I've always been afraid of you from that first day in the schoolhouse. I always knew that this day would come. I always feared you, and I always loved you, too."

THE END

About the Author

Max Brand is the best-known pen name of Frederick Faust, creator of Dr. Kildare, Destry, and many other fictional characters popular with readers and viewers worldwide. Faust wrote for a variety of audiences in many genres. His enormous output, totaling approximately thirty million words—the equivalent of five hundred thirty ordinary books—covered nearly every field: crime, fantasy, historical romance, espionage, Westerns, science fiction, adventure, animal stories, love, war, fashionable society, big business, and big medicine. Eighty motion pictures have been based on his work along with many radio and television programs. For good measure he also published four volumes of poetry. Perhaps no other author has reached more people in more different ways.

Born in Seattle in 1892, orphaned early, Faust grew up in the rural San Joaquin Valley of California. At Berkeley he became a student rebel and one-man literary movement, contributing prodigiously to all campus publications. Denied a degree because of unconventional conduct, he embarked on a series of adventures culminating in New York City where, after a period of near starvation, he received simultaneous recognition as a serious poet and successful author of fiction. Later, he traveled widely, making his home in New York, then in Florence, and finally in Los Angeles.

Once the United States entered the Second World War, Faust abandoned his lucrative writing career and his work as a screenwriter to serve as a war correspondent with the infantry in

Italy, despite his fifty-one years and a bad heart. He was killed during a night attack on a hilltop village held by the German army. New books based on magazine serials or unpublished manuscripts or restored versions continue to appear so that, alive or dead, he has averaged a new book every four months for seventy-five years. Beyond this, some work by him is newly reprinted every week of every year in one or another format somewhere in the world. A great deal more about this author and his work can be found in *The Max Brand Companion* (Greenwood Press, 1997) edited by Jon Tuska and Vicki Piekarski. His website is www.MaxBrandOnline.com.